VINCENT & EVE
BOOK TWO

RECKONING

JESSICA RUBEN

JessicaRubenBooks, LLC
229 E. 85th Street
P.O. Box 1596
New York, New York 10028

Copyright © 2018 Jessica Ruben
Paperback ISBN: 978-1-7321178-3-9
E-Book ISBN: 978-1-7321178-2-2
Printed in the United States of America

Contact me by visiting my website, JessicaRubenAuthor.com

Cover Art Design by Okay Creations
Formatting by A Book's Mind
Editing by Billi Joy Carson at Editing Addict
Editing by Ellie at LoveNBooks
Publicity by Autumn at Wordsmith Publicity

Except as permitted under the US Copyright Act of 1976, no part of this publication may be reproduced, distributed or transmitted in any form by any means, or stored in a database or retrieval system, without prior written permission of the author.

This is work of fiction. Names, characters, places, and incidents are the product of the author's wild imagination or are used fictitiously.

CONTENTS

Chapter 1 1

Chapter 2 9

Chapter 3 15

Chapter 4 43

Chapter 5 53

Chapter 6 57

Chapter 7 65

Chapter 8 73

Chapter 9 89

Chapter 10 99

Chapter 11 115

Chapter 12 117

Chapter 13 131

Chapter 14 133

Chapter 15 143

Chapter 16 149

Chapter 17 161

Chapter 18 177

Chapter 19 183
Chapter 20 185
Chapter 21 191
Chapter 22 203
Chapter 23 207
Chapter 24 217
Chapter 25 225
Chapter 26 227
Chapter 27 229
Chapter 28 231
Chapter 29 233
Acknowledgements 237

CHAPTER 1

EVE

My anxiety peaks as I listen to the sorority girls gossip about Vincent and his stunner of a girlfriend, Daniela. Vincent's past words ricochet around my mind… *"One foot in one world, one foot in another."* The doors of realization are now flung open, and there's no stopping the onslaught of truth. This man is Vincent Borignone, a member the largest crime family on the East Coast. He is also a student at one of the best colleges in the country. *"My entire life is duality,"* he said. My head throbs. I try to calm down by focusing on my immediate surroundings—starting with my table in the dining hall.

Claire, who I just met at the activity fair, sits on my right. With golden brown hair in a messy high bun, a light dusting of freckles on her nose, and a blue floral dress falling around her shoulders, she looks effortlessly beautiful. Her sorority sister—who I've nicknamed *Preppy-in-Pink* because I can't remember her name—sits on my left. The collar of her rose-colored Polo shirt is popped and a string of white pearls sit around her slender white neck; she blends in seamlessly with the blue-blood crowd of this Ivy League University.

The conversation gets loud again, and I can't help but listen in. My heart pounds into my stomach as the girls take a poll about whether or not sex with Vincent would be hot or scary as hell. They're likening him to a sexy vampire; a man everyone lusts after, but who may or may not take a vein. My mind is in overdrive as they all crack up with laughter. I need to get the hell out of here and look him up.

Ms. Levine's warnings ring in my ears. I should have done my research, but instead chose to stay in the dark. The truth is banging on my brain, echoing through every organ in my body. I jump out of my seat, interrupting their conversation with my unexpected movement. Claire and her friends stare at me in confusion.

"Sorry guys, I, um…uh…forgot something in my room," I blurt the excuse, trying not to stutter. I swivel my head to Claire. "Sorry, but I need to go." I turn to the rest of the group, my ponytail swinging. "It was nice to meet you all." I smile, but I'd bet it looks more like a grimace.

I drop down to the floor to grab my black backpack. Standing up too quickly, I smack the top of my head on the corner of the table. My eyes screw shut as I wonder what hurts more, the embarrassment or my skull.

Finally getting the nerve to reopen my eyes, I see the girls staring at me, trying not to laugh.

"Are you okay?" Claire's biting the side of her cheek. I resist the urge to rub the top of my head.

"I'm totally fine." My voice sounds higher pitched than usual.

She lets out a little chuckle. "Listen, we're all going out tomorrow night, maybe you wanna come with?"

I shuffle from one foot to the other, itching to go. "Um, sure. Text me?" I don't take another glance at the girls as I pivot, running to the front door like my ass is on fire.

At this point, I couldn't care less what they think. I just found out the man I thought I loved is Vincent Borignone, son of the biggest mafia Don on the East Coast. There's got to be some mistake. I get to the steps by the dining hall's entrance. Just as I'm about to leave, I pause.

Maybe I saw wrong.

Maybe that Vincent they're talking about isn't my Vincent.

I turn my head to get one last look. Even sitting down, I can see how much bigger he is than the boys around him. My eyes cover his ink-black hair styled in an undercut, his chiseled jaw beneath his high, widespread cheekbones, and his slight slant in the eyes, making him appear broody. The girls weren't wrong; he looks dangerous as all hell. I let out an involuntary groan as I spin back around, hightailing it out the door.

I'm jogging to my dorm room as my mind runs in circles. Sliding my backpack from my left to my right shoulder, I plunge my hand inside the small zipper pocket, searching for my phone. I pull out the first hard thing I feel, and it's a tube of Janelle's coconut lip balm. *Shit*! I stuff my hand back inside again and pull out my cell. I'm about to open my browser when I realize I need to calm down and do my research in the privacy of my room. I don't want to open this can in public, which will most likely be full of something worse than worms.

I know that what I'm about to see will probably annihilate me, but there can be no more hiding my head in the sand. Vincent's here and it's time I face the truth. I drop my phone back in my bag, trying to walk the rest of the way calmly. A few extra minutes won't mean anything.

I make it to my dorm room and fall into the chair at my desk. Flipping my laptop open and clicking on Firefox, I type in: Vincent Borignone. There are hundreds of photos of him with his girlfriend. *Holy shit*. My belly drops like a sack of cement.

I move my mouse through the images.

The first photo I see is Daniela in a tight white nurse's jacket, tits pushed up and pouring out. Her thin arms wrap themselves around Vincent's strong neck. She makes a kiss face to the camera, showcasing high cheekbones and full, blood-red lips. Vincent looks a bit rumpled like he hasn't shaved in a few days. Dressed in green doctor's scrubs, he's the sexy doctor to her overly styled nurse.

I continue scrolling through photographs, clicking on another one that catches my eye. The caption reads: WINTER WONDERLAND GALA. Daniela is in a long, pink sequin gown that pools by her feet. Vincent wears a gorgeous navy tux. It's dawning on me that they are socialites.

The next photograph is of the two of them at an event for poor inner-city children. The irony that I'm that poor inner-city child isn't lost on me. I continue to surf the internet, weirdly feeling like I'm researching a complete stranger.

After looking at hundreds of photographs, I enter the world of YouTube and click on a video of Vincent wrestling at Tri-Prep Academy. He's wearing a black singlet with a yellow lion on the front. I swallow hard, staring at every perfectly defined muscle in his body as he takes down his opponent. Raising my eyebrows, I take a look at his gigantic…package. My body immediately flushes. Why the hell did I never know how hot it is to watch guys wrestle? The crowd is going berserk when he wins. He looks up for a moment, and I can immediately tell that he was younger here. But still gorgeous.

My stalking knows no bounds as I read and watch anything and everything I can get my hands on. Columbia seems to have a gossip column of its own, *High and Low*, and Vincent and Daniela are on it weekly, spotted around campus like celebrities.

The first story I find is titled: "Vincent and Daniela, They're Just Like Us!" I assume it's a satire of *US Weekly* gossip magazine. Photo one shows them drinking coffee at a local cafe. The second shows him holding her hand, entering the mathematics center. The third has them at a back table of the library, books scattered around the desk while they study. The fourth has them in side-by-side photographs at the gym. On the left, he's bench-pressing a barbell. On the right, she's jogging on the treadmill. Her workout outfit is a white sports bra and matching white leggings with shiny stars.

Finally, I find a photo of Vincent with an older man at a charity. My throat tightens. He's with Antonio Borignone. They look so much alike; I can barely believe it. His father's eyes are electric blue, just as I remember from that day at the pawnshop. In fact, their physical similarity is so strong that it's almost ridiculous I didn't notice right away. Vincent is taller and more muscular, but he's his father's son.

I drop my head, forcing myself to see the truth. Vincent is the son of Antonio Borignone, the most notorious gangster on the East Coast. And his girlfriend looks like she's got the beauty of Grace Kelly and the brains of Einstein. I kick out my garbage can from beneath my desk, feeling like I'm going to puke. No. I'm stronger than that.

I move my hand back to my computer, staring at the most recent photo of them on *High and Low*. They're in the science lab conducting an experiment. Even with huge goggles and in front of a Bunsen burner, they look like perfection.

Finally, I pull out my cell phone and open up my Instagram account. Searching for his name, it's not difficult to find. His profile isn't private. I click on the first photo and see him drinking a beer on a yacht in Capri—tan chest and low-slung blue swim shorts. The next photo shows him training at a boxing gym in Bali with his shirt off. My body feels numb as I scan picture after picture, but when I glance at my fingers, I notice they're shaking. Moving back to the first picture, I see the last time he posted was a little over a year ago.

I check how many followers Vincent has. Two hundred thousand! And he's been silent for a year? Like a tempest, I feel a rush of anger and depression move through me. Clearly, I've been played. How could I have been so stupid to think that he would ever want me? And…how could I be even more stupid not to realize who he is?

I don't take a breath before I click on Daniela's name, tagged on one of Vincent's photos. I know that what I'm about to see will hurt me, but I'm on a masochistic binge right now, knifing myself with truth. For some reason, I feel as if I need to see all of this. I want to make sure that my brain, heart, and body all understand that whatever I thought I had with Vincent is good and done.

Finally clicking on her name, I see she has one point four million followers. I look at hundreds of photos, dissecting each and every detail. Her entire feed is about New York City glamour and travel. Even the mundane shit she does is perfect. In one photo, she's eating a hot dog in Central Park with her tiny little white dog on a leash. In another, she's strutting across a New York City street in sky-high heels and a cropped fur jacket.

In another picture, she's wearing a long, silver gown and hanging on the arm of the sexiest man alive—Vincent—for an event, Feed the Children. I read the comments.

BeachnSand472: Who makes your gown? LOVE!
PebblesnRox: You guys are perfect!

SheRaines: please grab his ass for me!

DocAllie: OMG! #GoalsAF

Jay_Har4572: DYINGGGGG. Love love love!

Candybaby999: OBSESSEDDDDDD need that dress, AND that man.

Fashon4more: He's hot AF!

Janananana: #couplegoals

Another photo. Daniela dives off a yacht, her pink bikini sparkling under the sunlight. Her caption: ST. BARTHS WITH BAE. Vincent's watching her with a smile on his face as if he can't believe how beautiful she is. Did he ever look at me like that?

I move to another photo and see them at the Robin Hood Gala, raising money to combat New York City homelessness.

Caption:

Enjoying a special night with the love of my life. #MileyCyrus #Coldplay #stophomelessness #lovemycity #bestmanever #heartofgold #goodcause #charity #giving #robinhood

I do a quick Google search and see that tables for this event start at over ten thousand dollars.

I move back to Instagram, staring at another photo of Daniela at the Robin Hood Gala. She's posing with a girl who looks just like her, but with blonde hair instead of auburn. The girl's name is tagged and I click, finding myself on Daniela's sister's page.

The first photo I check is in the middle of her feed. A group of friends smile around a huge white Christmas tree, decorated in what looks like hundreds of gold and silver ornaments. The caption: CHRISTMAS IN VERMONT! Enlarging the photo with my thumb and forefinger, I spot Vincent smiling in the background in a black sweater and jeans. Considering how tall he is, the tree must be over seven feet! My heart constricts; I've never seen a tree this perfect in my life.

I remember all the years Janelle and I would celebrate Christmas a week late, so we could take someone's old tree from the dumpster. I'd string Fruit Loops on a colorful lanyard, while Janelle would put a knot at either end so the cereal wouldn't slide off. And then I'd sit on her shoulders and scatter our stringed cereal around the tree. My eyes prickle with tears, remembering how beautiful and special I thought it was. Meanwhile, I was nothing but a poor gutter rat living in the ghetto with a big sister who tried to make it right. I swallow the thought as I read Daniela's sister's hashtags:

#après ski #sorrynotsorry #cheers #kissesunderthemistletoe #dontbejealous #lifeisgood

After finding myself on Daniela's sister's boyfriend's page, I know I've gotten out of hand. I shut my phone off because I don't trust myself not to go back for more. I sprawl out on my bed, shaking my feet until my shoes pop off. My eyes burn from staring at my phone for so long.

I should study. Read. I need to compartmentalize this and keep my focus on school. In fact, I should be happy all of this unfolded because it makes it clear that whatever we had is ancient history. Part of me wants to die, but another part of me wants to show his ass up. I never want to feel like this again. And I refuse to ever be that girl I used to be; I was naïve and stupid.

I spend the rest of my night with my eyes glued to my books, hoping if I just study hard enough, I can push the Vincent shit to the back of my head. I went through hell and back to be where I am, and I won't let a man stop me from succeeding.

With the help of the school's guidance counselor, I've already planned out my path to becoming an attorney like I've always dreamed. The possibility of a safe and secure future, complete with money in the bank, is so close I can practically taste it. As far as I'm concerned, nothing else matters. Vincent Borignone can go to hell.

CHAPTER 2

VINCENT

The fall semester began last week, and I've got a shitload of work to get done in addition to work for the family. Unfortunately, I'm stuck sitting here at Maison Kayser, a fancy French coffee shop on the Upper East Side. Daniela snootily orders four different desserts and a skim-milk cappuccino from the waiter, requesting the shape of a heart in the foam.

This restaurant actually pays Daniela to eat here—just so she'll take a picture of her enjoying the food and post it on the internet. Apparently, millions of girls all over the world look up to Daniela and want to eat where she eats. Last week, she posted a photograph of her lip gloss, and within an hour, the color was sold out almost everywhere.

"Y-yes, miss." The waiter stumbles over his words before scurrying away. She smiles like an evil cat; Daniela loves to make people fidget.

"You know, Vincent." She presses her overly plumped lips together, shifting forward to get closer to me. "The whole-milk cappuccino looks a lot more beautiful than the skim one. I feel like the color is whiter. I wonder if there's anything to that theory?" She looks at me expectantly, tilting her head to the side. She's put some shimmer or some shit on her cheeks, and it makes her face sparkle.

I stare at her but refuse to answer such a dumb question.

"Waiter," she calls out, not taking her green eyes off mine. She lifts her hand in the air, shifting her fingers around like an impatient child.

He walks back over to us. Before he can take out his pad and a pen, she barks her updated order. "I want a skim and whole-milk cappuccino." Her demanding attitude grates on my nerves. "And I'm in a hurry. Have them rush it."

I finally break my hatred-fueled eye contact to look at the waiter, stopping him before he can walk away. "Thank you." He nods at me appreciatively before leaving.

She snickers at the angry look on my face. "Oh, come on, Vincent. It's his job."

I shake my head slowly. "The way you treat people, Daniela."

"Oh, come on. You're the richest man in this place. Don't be so sour."

"Sour? What does money have to do with anything. You have no respect for anyone. All you care about is your social media bullshit."

"Don't talk down to me," she spits. "Social media is the new age."

"No one gives a fuck!"

"They don't? Tell that to my million followers or the designers who beg me to wear their clothes and accessories." She pulls out a green cashmere sweater from a shopping bag hanging off her seat. "Tell that to this gorgeous sweater you've been gifted by Armani. People would die to get this for free."

"I'm not wearing your shit." I crack my knuckles one at a time. "You ask me all the time, and the answer is always the same—*no*. You need me to come out, smile for a damn photograph, fine. But wearing the clothes you choose? Fuck no." I clench my jaw and she immediately pulls back.

She drops her lips into a frown. I can sense she's going to try a new tactic. Daniela is nothing if not a great actress.

"Vincent, you don't have to wear any of it, okay?" Her voice is five times higher than it was a moment ago, her eyes spelling out disappointment. But I know the only real thing behind her gaze is calculation.

I let out a cutting laugh. "I'm not your bitch, Daniela. I never will be. I don't wear what you tell me to wear. I do what I want, when I want. Feel me? I may be stuck in this fucking lie of a relationship to keep your father happy, but remember that you and I are nothing in real life. Don't delude yourself into thinking otherwise."

She tries to put her hand on mine, but I tear it away before she can touch me.

"I know, baby. Calm down. You're too wound up. It's because classes have started, right? I know how serious you get about school." She looks around, making sure no one is watching us argue, the idea that anyone might see us gets her nervous. "Tell me what I can do to relax you, huh?" She licks the corner of her lip seductively.

I practically snarl. "You've got to be kidding me." I throw my napkin on the table and push my chair back, wanting to get the hell away from her.

"Come on," she purrs with a gleam in her eye. "I know we haven't fucked in ages, but it doesn't mean you can't change your mind—"

I grip the side of the table, my knuckles turning white. "I will *never* touch you again, understand?" I take a deep breath, doing my best not to flip the table and walk out. Luckily, the waiter brings the two cappuccinos and a tray full of gourmet desserts, none of which she plans to eat. I've actually watched her take bites of food only to spit it out after the photograph has been taken.

The waiter glances at my hardened face and drops the dishes in front of us before speed-stepping to the back of the room.

"But why, Vincent? We were so good together!"

"No. We weren't."

"We used to fuck like crazy! You loved it. I know you did. I just don't understand—"

"My life isn't for you to understand," I growl in frustration. She can't take a hint.

She sits up with her lips pursed, knowing no matter how much I hate her guts, I'm not going anywhere. "Anyway, sit back. I don't want your shadow in the pictures. Oh, actually, do you think you'll eat a dessert for me? I think everyone would love to see you opening wide for something white and creamy." She raises her brows, smirking. Does she think she's funny?

I breathe hard, trying not to tear the hair from her skull. "You're a sick bitch. You know that?"

"If I remember clearly, it didn't bother you too much before. In fact, I think you liked it."

Daniela Costa is into some kinky shit—and that's saying a lot coming from a man like me, who has done it all, and then some. When we started out, I was nothing but a cocky kid, willing to lay it on her for two reasons: one, she was hot; two, the family wanted someone to keep a close eye on the business we had with her father—owner of the largest bank in Central America. Costa houses and cleans our dirty money. Daniela and I went to school together, and it was damn obvious she wanted my dick. It was no surprise my father tapped me on the back to handle it.

We all hate Alexander Costa, and everyone knows he's a loose cannon, but there really isn't another option to working with him. Not yet, at least. As our operations continue to grow and give off cash, the small-time pawnshops and strip clubs aren't enough to launder all of our money. Costa, on the other hand, has the capacity to clean tens of millions a year. The situation seemed easy; I fucked Daniela, kept an eye on business, and all was well.

And then I met Eve. She's genuine and smart and somehow, perfect for me. She just got me. The real me.

I knew I couldn't touch Daniela anymore. It's not that I was ever faithful to her and she easily accepted it. Once I met someone real, the thought of another woman wasn't appealing anymore. Simple as that.

I spoke to the family, letting them know business dealings between Costa and the family were functioning well, and we had no reason to keep such a close eye on him anymore. The man was making a huge percentage off our business; none of us thought he'd be dumb enough to jeopardize that kind of cash flow. But when I made it clear to Daniela that she and I were done, she went insane. I don't think anyone in her life has ever told her "no" before.

It took only an hour for Costa to call my father and go berserk, threatening the family. Keeping his princess Daniela happy was necessary, or he'd stop laundering and holding our cash. Apparently, she was in the midst of growing her social media empire, and my face was essential to her growing fame. A family vote was called, and everyone insisted I make it right with her. I was told to do whatever it takes to keep her happy. That is, until I build a new business to take over Costa's use of ours.

I've spent this past year working to build out my own hotel and casino complex on the Tribal Lands in Nevada. As the son of a Masuki Tribe member, I have some inalienable rights, which I plan to capitalize on. And if the numbers turn how I expect them to? Our dirty cash can easily be laundered within the hundreds of millions we'll be making per year in clean money.

Once I get the family out of Costa's grip, I'll be free of him and his leech daughter. And then, maybe, I can find Eve again.

The terms between Daniela and me right now are simple: I have to look and act as though I'm still with her. She doesn't care whether or not we fuck anymore, so long as I play the part. But if I refuse to smile for the damn camera? She'll get Daddy involved, and the family would be left with a boatload of cash that the FBI would love to get their hands on. I'm stuck being her public boyfriend until Gaming gets off the ground.

Daniela shifts a bony shoulder and shuffles in her seat, bringing my attention back to her. "I think the red raspberries look best against the white cup, don't you?" She moves the cappuccino slightly askew and snaps maybe twenty pictures of each dessert with the frothy drink. Standing up to get other angles, her jeans hug her flat ass. How do millions of girls look up to this shit?

Daniela stops taking pictures, putting her fancy iPhone down on the table and bringing the cappuccino up to her glossy lips. "Okay. Talk to me. What's going on, Vincent? You're brooding and more pissed-off than usual." She rolls her eyes, putting down her cup.

I clench my teeth. "Just take the fucking photo already." We both know why I'm here today, and it isn't to chitchat.

"Okay, if you insist." She smiles. "Turn to the side and lean back on the chair with your foot crossed at the front."

The flash goes off and I grind my teeth together.

CHAPTER 3

EVE

The next morning, I decide I will do everything in my power to forget Vincent goes to school here. I do my best to focus on starting my day, one small step at a time. After washing up and getting dressed, I take a quick trip to the dining hall for a gigantic coffee and a bagel. Bringing the food back to my desk and sitting quietly to eat, I do my best not to get any crumbs on the floor. Finally, I crack open my economics textbook.

My room is a simple square, located on the third floor of one of the old gothic buildings making up the freshman quad. The desk next to mine is empty; I was supposed to have a roommate, but she decided last minute to defer admission for a year. After living in the Blue Houses—where I could hear my neighbor's conversations and smell everyone's cooking twenty-four seven—this room has become my own little sanctuary.

Staring at the supply-and-demand curve, I again reread the same passage. I need this shit to make sense! I drop my head on my desk and groan. It's only ten in the morning, and I already feel tired.

And then, like a three-dimensional puzzle with a gaping hole in the center, my brain finds the missing piece and places it right where it belongs. "Oh, thank God!" I exclaim out loud. "I understand! I get it!"

I jump up from my chair, dancing to music that isn't on, shaking my ass left to right. My phone *buzzes* mid-dance, and I smile wide when I see it's Claire. After my weird stunt yesterday, I was worried she'd write me off.

Claire: Meet me at my dorm @ 10. Brearley Houses. Come earlier if you want to pre-game!

Me: I'm planning on studying today, not sure if I'll be feeling up to going out later. Can I text you?

Claire: Come on, girl! We'll have fun! Come out!

I look back at the economics book. I deserve to go out, right? I promised Janelle last week that I'd do my best to get out more at night. Now that I'm living in relative safety, I don't have to be a hermit. And, while it's hard to change my old ways, it's something I'm consciously trying to modify about myself.

"You know what?" I exclaim loudly into my empty room. "I'm going out."

Me: Okay. I'll be there. See you later!

The day goes by with my head in the books, my only break to run down to the campus deli to pick up a turkey sandwich and another large coffee.

By evening, my brain feels completely fried. I lift my hands to my hair and try to pull the rubber band from my ponytail. When it gets caught in a knot, I whimper, trying to pull it free. I finally remove it, but not without ripping out a bunch of hairs in the process. Ouch.

Looking at my old worn-out clothing, I take stock of my situation. I seriously need to revive myself if I'm going to be seen in public tonight. I quickly undress, slide on my blue robe and Old Navy flip-flops, and grab my lime-green shower caddy. Peeking out of my door to make sure the hallway is clear, I sprint to the girl's bathroom, praying with each step that I won't bump into someone. I know it's only girls on this floor, but I'm self-conscious about being seen in nothing other than a terry-cloth bathrobe.

After shaving and scrubbing as best as I can, I grab the fancy shampoo Janelle brought me from her swanky salon and massage my scalp with my fingertips. I inhale, smelling the creamy coconut scent. After rinsing, I take out the conditioner and let it sit in my hair for three-minutes, exactly as the instructions suggest. I'm standing and waiting for the time to pass when I hear a few girls walking into the bathroom, giggling.

"…saw them at the business center!"

"I seriously can't even—"

"You can't?" another voice interrupts. "Well, I can! Doesn't Vincent look like he'd be a total savage in bed? God, I bet he fucks like—"

Laughter.

I hear a swishing sound in my ears. I want to turn away, pretend that I didn't just hear his name in the context of sex with someone, but I can't un-hear the words.

Their high-pitched voices taper off until I hear the door *clang* shut.

My face contorts into an ugly cry. No sound is coming out of my mouth, but the silent moans wrack my chest. Tears run furiously down my face, mingling with the shower water. My heart moves low into my stomach, my mother's voice barging into the forefront of my mind. She's railing. I can hear her words echoing against my skull. *"You're nothing! A zero!"*

I lean my hands against my knees under the spray, trying not to heave as my stomach twists. I slightly turn my head and come face to face with my beautiful shampoo bottle. Even with Janelle's salon discount, it was still crazy expensive. But, she wanted me to go to school with "good hair." According to her, it would help me do better in my classes. Somehow, I manage a small chuckle along with my tears. Then Angelo forces himself into my mind, too. Angelo, who thinks I'm destined for great things. They're the scaffolding to the strong and independent woman I want to become. I need to lean on their opinions of me, and not let some asshole tear me down.

I put my hands back to my sides and stand taller. I rinse my hair, and with as much strength as I can muster, open the shower curtain and put my robe back on. Gathering my wits, I leave the bathroom with my head held high.

After getting into my room, I slide on an old band T-shirt that one of Janelle's ex-boyfriends gave her. I conveniently took it along with a few other items before moving out because, well, sisters! I take out my blow-dryer and a round brush, placing it on my desk while I separate my hair into sections, drying my hair piece by piece, just as Janelle taught me.

I look in my mirror, relieved that I managed to turn thick dark hair into something relatively smooth. I drop the brush at my desk, exclaiming, "Fuck love!" Better yet, fuck Vincent Borignone! I'm going to work as hard as I can while I'm here, and I'm not allowing a man to take advantage of me again. I'm a freshman with my head in the books, and it seems that he's the most notorious bad boy on campus. Why would our paths ever cross? They shouldn't. And thank God for that. I couldn't bear for him to see me. Would he laugh? I'm sure he would. I was so stupid.

I pull out a pair of tight black jeans and a simple white tank from the top from my closet. Sliding on a stack of gold bangles I bought from H&M, I finish myself off with some clear lip gloss and a little mascara. I feel casual, but a hell of a lot better than I did an hour ago.

I'm no longer that pathetic girl who hides behind her sister and her books. I'm new. I'm improved. And Vincent Borignone can kiss. My. Ass. At the end of the day, all that shit is behind me. It's done. And I'm… over it!

Like a horrible thunderstorm, memories of the two of us flash through my head. But this time, I inject my newfound knowledge into every past moment. We met at the fight, but he was with Daniela—who probably gave him a blowjob in the bathroom. He brought me to the skating rink, but he likely went home that same night to Daniela, who was waiting for him, wearing nothing but sexy black lingerie and high fuck-me heels. He took me to pizza but shot those Russians in the head while Pauli distracted me with conversation!

The Borignone mafia is nothing if not arrogant and powerful. Just last month, I read a newspaper article about an explosion killing an FBI agent and his wife in their car. Apparently, this agent was garnering evidence to bring forward a case against the Borignone mafia. And Vincent is part of this? I shake my head side to side, disgusted that I ever touched him. I vaguely wonder what part he plays. Is he simply a soldier at the lowest rung? No way. He's too intelligent for that. Maybe he's one of the Capo who reports to the boss? Even that feels like it isn't enough. As the son of Antonio, I have no doubt that he plays a crucial role in their sick schemes.

I grab the small black bag Janelle bought for me as a graduation gift, filling it with some essentials: lip gloss, cell phone, my ID, and some cash. I leave my room, taking the steps to the lobby. Pushing open the building's large wooden front door, I inhale the scent of flowers. The campus is simply beautiful and perfectly maintained—an oasis in the city.

I take my time walking to Claire's. Even though it's evening, the entire school is lit up with huge streetlamps. I pause to read a silver engraved plaque located on the back of a wooden bench: IN LOVING MEMORY OF DAN BROWNING, WHO ALWAYS LIKED TO SIT. I chuckle, rolling my eyes to high heaven. These rich people have so much money, and they spend it on this shit? I shake my head at the absurdity of it all and finish my short walk to Claire's dorm.

"Hey," the guy at the front desk stares at his phone intently. "Who are you here for?" His hair is long in the front and covers most of his eyes.

"I'm waiting for Claire, um, I'm not sure her last name. But she's a sophomore."

He finally lifts his head and pauses, his mouth hanging slightly open and cheeks turning pink. I look down at my clothes, self-consciously wondering if there's something wrong with me.

"Do you want to w-wait here, or go up?" His eyes flicker between my eyes, lips, and boobs.

"Uh, I'll just wait here," I mumble, pulling my tank higher to cover me better. I take a seat in one of the lobby's plastic chairs, typing out a message to Claire that I'm waiting downstairs.

I try to relax. I'm still unsure about the best way to cope with this new world. It's hard enough to sit in class with these entitled rich kids, but it's even harder to have to go out socially and try to act like I'm the same as they are. In my heart, I'm still the poor girl from the ghetto. I know technically, I've left my old life behind—I'm a student here, just like everyone else. But still, the past remains with me. The result is a sense of not really belonging anywhere. Maybe if I just pretend to be like them for long enough, my new persona will become me. Eve Petrov, Columbia-educated woman. Eve Petrov, attorney-at-law. I like the sound of that.

I look back up again at the guy sitting at the front desk. He doesn't look much older than I am. I once read that every passerby has a life as vivid and complex as my own. I wonder if that could possibly be true. He looks like any other preppy white kid, but then again, he's working here tonight instead of chugging beers at a frat house.

Claire walks out of the elevator. She looks beautiful in a fitted jean jacket and a long black cotton dress with a high slit in the thigh. Her outfit is casual but still manages to show off her toned body. When we look at each other, I feel a combination of relief and happiness. I know we've only just met, but it feels like we could be good friends.

"Hey, girl! I'm glad you decided to come out." Her voice is upbeat. I stand from the chair, and we head out into the night.

"Where are all of your friends?" I rub my hands up and down my arms. Since I left my dorm, it seems that the weather has dropped fifteen degrees.

"They may meet us there later," Claire replies. "It's just the two of us for now. Oh, by the way, the party is close, so we can walk. Totally beats having to get in a cab, right? Maybe we should go downtown to a bar in the West Village later if the party here sucks. Did you bring an ID by any chance?" Her voice is hopeful.

I nod my head, relieved that my age won't cause a problem. "Yeah. My sister called the DMV over the summer and told them she lost her driver's license, so they sent her a new one and I got to keep her old."

"Oh my God, that's so lucky! Mine is just one of the older girls in Phi Alpha, and she looks nothing like me!" We laugh.

Even though we didn't drive, Janelle thought it was important for us to have driver's licenses. Somehow, she got Vania's brother to lend us his old Volvo once a week so we could practice.

Claire and I finally get off campus. Everywhere I turn, college students are ignoring traffic signals, or running drunkenly from one corner to the next. A group of girls, all in short skirts, walk ahead of us.

Finally, we enter a small but obviously expensive-looking building. The uniformed doorman nods to us as we walk into the elevator. Claire pushes the button for the penthouse level and we smile at each other excitedly. The door opens directly into a huge loft. Claire immediately steps out, but it takes me a second to realize this is the party.

Hard-core rap music blares on the speakers. I step inside, doing my best to give off a casual vibe as if this social scene doesn't scare me. But the truth is everything around me serves as a reminder that I'm out of place. Floor-to-ceiling glass windows and an open floor plan give the apartment an airy feel. The walls are filled with beautiful black-and-white photography, framed in silver and gold. This place screams money.

I turn my head to see a green ping-pong table along the wall by the kitchen. Some people are playing a drinking game on it, throwing balls into cups on the opposite side of the table. There's a beautiful brown leather sectional couch in the center of the room. A coffee table is littered with ashtrays, red cups, and empty water bottles. Random pockets of students grind their bodies together to the music.

Before saying hello to anyone, Claire walks us into a large chrome and silver kitchen. Bottles of alcohol are spread out chaotically across a white marble island. She checks them out and finally picks up a magnum of vodka that's already half empty. She pours some into two large plastic cups, adding some Diet Pepsi to each. After handing one to me, and taking the other for herself, we walk to the side of the living room. Clinking our drinks together, we take our first sips. The swallow burns, but I do my best not to flinch.

"To new friends," she says.

"New friends." My heart actually warms in my chest.

Claire checks her phone while I look around the party. I put my lips back onto the cup's rim when I lock eyes across the room with a familiar guy. He's big and built, but also really preppy looking. It only takes a moment for me to realize that we're both staring at each other questioningly, trying to place the other. Wait. Is this who I think it is? Oh. My. God. Does he remember meeting me? Vincent introduced me to him the night of the underground fight in the Meatpacking District. Did Vincent ever tell him about us? Does he know anything? Is he also Borignone mafia?

He starts to move through the crowd, seemingly toward me.

My heart thumps.

Some girl stops him to say hello and he barely gives her a second glance. He's on his way.

He reaches his destination—me. Standing tall and naturally imposing, I'd peg him at over six feet tall, and in this moment, I'm wishing I wore a pair of higher heels. I feel like a kid in front of this man.

"Holy shit," he says, not unkindly. "You're Eve." His lips quirk up into a smile, but I can tell there are nerves behind his relaxed demeanor.

"Do you know Claire?" I point to her, deflecting. His eyes smile as he takes her in.

"Of course, I do."

Claire rolls her eyes as if she's been there and done that. "Yeah," she says. "I know Tom." She cocks her head to the side and crosses her arms over her chest, full of attitude. He doesn't look daunted.

"Oh, come on, Claire," he laughs. "We had some fun together, didn't we?"

"Huh," she says skeptically. "I vaguely remember sitting in the dining hall with the rest of my pledge class when we all got a text on our phone at the same time." Claire's face is reddening, but Tom looks like he's trying not to laugh.

"And you wouldn't believe it, Eve, but, it was the same exact message. From the same guy. And do you know what this text said to each and every one of us?"

I let my gaze bounce between the two of them.

"It said"—she lifts her hands to make air quotes—"Netflix and chill?"

Tom breaks out into laughter. "Come on—I was throwing out an option and figured someone would respond! How was I supposed to know you were all together?"

"We were all pledging Phi Alpha! We were together for the entire semester, you moron."

"All right, so I got busted. Doesn't mean you and I didn't have fun while it lasted though, right?"

I want to ask if Vincent is here, but I don't have the nerve. Tom glances toward the couch. I turn my eyes and—there he is, facing away from me while Daniela straddles his lap. The back of his head rests against the cushion while she grinds up against him to the music.

I turn away, trying not to stare. Tom looks at me with pity in his eyes and all at once, I feel like crying. He must know everything. I wish I could care less about this right now. Against all odds, I made it to one of the best schools in the country. I have everything paid for and taken care of. My sister is safe. I'm safe. I have a nice clean bedroom to sleep in every night. I'm on a path to success. I can't let this bother me.

Still, seeing them in front of my face feels like I'm receiving punishment for a crime I never committed. I need to get out of here before Vincent sees me. The last thing on earth I want right now is to bump into him while he's with his girlfriend.

Tom seems to notice my distress. He shrugs his shoulders as if to say that what I'm witnessing is just the normal course of things.

"You girls want another drink? Eve, you look like you could use one."

"We just got," Claire replies, lifting her full cup. "But I could use a bottle of water."

Tom nods. "No problem. Let me grab one for you." He turns, walking toward the kitchen.

Claire's eyes follow Tom as he saunters off. "Ugh, he is such a man-whore. Then again, we did have a lot of fun together."

"Yeah," I reply, taking another huge gulp of my drink. If she's still talking, I wouldn't know. I need an exit strategy, stat.

Claire turns her head toward Vincent and Daniela. "He's best friends with Vincent. That guy, over there." She points to his back. "I know Vincent's gorgeous, but he's so intense. I don't know what it is about him, but he always looks so aggressive…so, dominant. I obviously get the appeal, but sometimes he just like, scares the shit out of me."

"Tom looks pretty intense, too," I add.

"Yeah, but not in the same way. Tom is sort of free-spirited; he messes around and makes a lot of jokes. He's definitely got that aggressive side too, but not like Vincent. Vincent is like, brilliant. And huge. And rough." She laughs, taking another sip of her drink. "They say he got a full scholarship, even though he's a gazillionaire!"

"Oh." I shrug and take a deep breath, my gaze falling back on the asshole who cared for me—during my lowest moments—like no one else. I need to hold myself together, at least until I find somewhere private to cry.

A girl I've never met before walks over to Claire. "Do you see the bag Daniela has?" She's huffing, annoyance written all over her pale face. "How the hell did she even find it? I looked everywhere for that bag and it was sold out! Barneys, Bergdorf, Net-a-Porter, everywhere!"

I've recently come to understand that in this rich people's world—where everyone has the money, the looks, and the intellect—connections and access are what reign supreme. Because when everyone can afford the newest "it" bag, it's no longer exciting or special to have it. The goal becomes about having a bag that others can't get their hands on.

"Who cares? I think it's ugly anyway," Claire looks at me and winks. "By the way Alexa, this is Eve. Eve, this is Alexa. She's a junior in Phi Alpha."

Alexa turns to me, giving a genuine smile. "Nice to meet you. Are you planning to rush?"

"Oh, I don't know. Maybe?" I lift a shoulder in question.

"You totally should. We have a lot of fun and it's great to have a smaller community within the college scene. Especially since the city is so huge, you know? It's good to have that close-knit family feeling."

She turns her body again to face Claire. "A few of us are heading over to another party in the building next door. Come with?"

"We just got here. I think we'll stay for a bit." The girls air-kiss goodbye and Alexa waves to me as she walks away.

Claire plunges a hand into her huge purse, searching for something. "I almost forgot!" She pulls out two small bags of pretzels and hands one to me. "I brought these for us so we won't get too drunk tonight. Carbs to soak up the alcohol!"

I take the pretzels from her hand, feeling like crying even harder now. The fact that she thought of me enough to bring this little snack is beyond thoughtful. I've never really had anyone in my life other than Janelle who I could call a friend. And in this moment, Claire is seriously coming close to that mark.

Tom walks back over with a bottle of Poland Spring and within seconds, they're shamelessly flirting. I drop the pretzels into my bag and hold my drink in a death grip as my eyes move back to Vincent and Daniela. I just can't stop myself; watching him with her is like staring at an awful car crash. It's sickening to see, but impossible to turn from.

Apparently, I'm not the only one with a staring problem because Daniela's stripper dance is beginning to garner interest. Katy Perry and Rihanna's "Black Horse" booms on the speakers as a few preppy-looking guys move closer together, hooting and hollering as she grinds on Vincent. It's obvious she's loving all of the attention she's getting; her seductive dancing only increases with their cheers. Her narrow hips slowly circle as her long auburn hair sways down her back. The look in her eyes is seduction.

She spins around in an expert-looking move. While the front of her top was relatively modest, the back is entirely open and strung together with nothing other than a few delicate gold chains. The shirt showcases her milky-white skin. I wish I could see Vincent's face, but he's still sitting looking away from me.

Daniela finally moves off him when the music changes. I know it's not rational, but I feel instantly relieved. Some of the guys who were watching start to boo, begging her to keep dancing. She demurely shrugs as if she didn't even realize anyone was watching her. "Oh, please," I say under my breath.

Meanwhile, Vincent leans forward on the couch, seemingly ignoring everyone and focusing on a muted UFC match on the big-screen TV in front of him. I step closer to Tom and Claire. Strangely, it feels like Tom keeps darting his eyes toward me. He's not giving off any sexual interest, but he is for sure watching me.

I glance back to see Daniela walking toward her friends. Pulling out a phone from her bag, she leans into the group with her arm extended forward, posing for selfies.

I subconsciously lift my tank top higher, making sure I'm not showing too much skin. I let out a groan of irritation. I'm sick and tired of the same old issues that I've always had—the same boring flaws and anxieties that have been gnawing at me for years. Every girl here is dressed sexy and I can, too. I'm in college, a place for reinvention within relative safety. I have nothing to fear anymore. I pull my tank down just a bit so that the top of my breasts show. *There!*

All of a sudden, Daniela and her friends turn to me together. *Oh, shit.* They totally caught me staring. I do a quick about-face and try to act like I'm part of the conversation between Claire and Tom.

I feel a soft hand on my back and I immediately flinched, turning around.

"Didn't mean to scare you," Daniela says with a saccharine smile. "Having fun?" Her perfectly plucked auburn eyebrows are raised in question.

I want to look happy, but my face won't move. Luckily, Claire turns to us then, her presence immediately breaking the potential for awkwardness. Tom casually drapes an arm around Daniela's thin shoulder and pulls her in for a hug. Of course, they're friends. This is his best friend's girlfriend.

"How was your summer, Claire?" she asks as she relaxes comfortably into Tom's side. She sounds just as a rich girl would: confident and perfectly measured. Claire, who I could swear was slouching just a moment ago, is now standing ramrod straight with her stomach pulled in and shoulders back.

"It was great. I was working in Malawi actually." She glances down for a moment before resuming eye contact.

"I always knew you were one of those do-gooder types. You're pre-med, right?"

"Yeah," Claire says proudly. "Did you declare your major?"

"Yeah. I'm business." Her voice is upbeat. "I plan to work with my father's bank after graduation; so this works for me."

I hate that she has a brain. If she were stupid, I'd feel a whole lot better about this entire conversation right now. I stand silently, hoping that everyone just forgets I exist.

Unfortunately, I have no such luck. Daniela turns her face toward mine, placing a hand on her chest. "I'm Daniela by the way." Pointing to a group of girls who are now standing behind her, she introduces them next. "This is Allie, Jenna, and Julie." She turns to another girl standing slightly behind them. "Oh, and that's Quinn."

"Hi!" they all reply in unison. I eye each one of them, their hair all long and highlighted in the same honey-blonde shade. The girls stand around Daniela as if they're her secretaries, ready to do her bidding at a moment's notice.

Daniela's smile is back on me. "You should take a look at Omega Chi during rush next semester." She looks me up and down, assessing me. "You're so pretty. I feel like you would really fit in with us." I blink a few times nervously, feeling confused. I know she's speaking English, but it's as if there's an undercurrent to her words that I can't catch onto.

"So, what's your name?" she asks expectantly.

I clear my throat, hoping that I can get a word out. "Eve." I rub my sweaty palms on my thighs, wishing she'd leave me alone.

She nods her head slightly as if my name is suitable to her. "Well, we're all about to head out. This party totally sucks. But I'm so glad we met. See you soon, Eve." She struts off in her black stiletto heels, her posse walking behind her.

The moment they're gone, I lean back against the wall, looking for support. Claire is about to say something when I interrupt her. "Do you know where the bathroom is?"

"It's in the back, second door to the left," Tom replies with a piercing gaze. Does he think I'm going to steal something? Jeez.

Before I walk away, Claire gives me a face like *holy shit I can't believe Daniela was here just now*, but then looks back at Tom to continue chatting. I walk away from them, moving as quickly as I can. For a moment, I wonder if I should turn around and leave the party. But Daniela may be in the lobby, waiting for a ride or something. I don't want to bump into her.

Luckily, I find the bathroom quickly and walk right inside, locking the door behind me. It's small, white, and thankfully still clean. I put my hands on either side of the sink and bow my head, my breathing labored. How long should I stay in here?

I finally lift my face and look at my reflection. My hair, which I painstakingly straightened a few hours ago, now has a wave to it and my face is flushed, lips puffy. I look down at my wrist and find a skinny black hair tie. Pulling my hair back in a tight bun, I immediately feel better. Turning on the faucet, I put my wrists under the ice-cold water, trying to cool my body down. I feel completely depleted from seeing Vincent and meeting Daniela. All I want to do is run back to my dorm room and cry myself to sleep.

What I need to do is leave this party. I let out a whimper and stare at myself hard, willing the tears not to leave my eyes. Everything with Vincent was blown up in my childish mind. He has his own life, and I was nothing more than his little sideshow. What a joke I must have been. A pathetic joke. I'm going to walk back into the party and tell Claire that I have a terrible headache. Hopefully, I'll be able to find her quickly and without incident.

I hear a knock on the bathroom door. "Just a s-second." I try to stop my voice from stammering. I take a few deep breaths when I hear another hard bang.

"Just a minute!" I yell again, my voice stronger. I stare at myself, trying to muster the strength to go back outside.

"Whoever is fuckin' in there, better get out." It's a man on the other side, his voice deep and angry. I turn around, swinging the door open with annoyance. What a jerk!

A huge body looms in front of me. We lock eyes, both rooted to our respective spots. The plot of my life just doesn't make sense anymore.

"Eve?" The tone of his voice registers that he's completely stunned. He puts his hands on either side of the doorframe, seemingly to steady himself.

"Uh..." My entire brain goes on mute as I drop my head and stare at dark denim hugging muscular thighs, my eyes track upward to a tight black T-shirt that stretches across a wide chest, and finally, my eyes lock with a dark and penetrating gaze that belongs to only one man.

"Eve?" he repeats. While I didn't think it would be possible, his stare deepens. All I can process is how vulnerable I feel in this moment. When Vincent looks at me, it's as if he can see within me. It's exposure I both yearn for and despise.

In a blink, he steps inside and locks the door behind him. He bends down and lifts me onto the counter, dropping his head in my neck and breathing me in. My legs immediately spread apart to make room for him to get closer. He wraps his huge hands on either side of my head, keeping me in place while he lowers his head to look straight at me again as if to confirm that I'm real.

"You're here? But, how—" his voice breaks off. I listen to his shallow breaths mixed with mine.

Seeing him face to face like this brings it all back in a rush. He's so *intense*. I swallow hard. How much time passes with us locked in the bathroom like this, I have no idea. I'm lost to him. All of my pain and anger seems to have gone up in smoke. I want to stay lost in his eyes and simply savor this moment and the way he's looking at me.

He keeps his hands on the sides of my face, thumbs gently rubbing my temples. It's soothing and arousing. I'd clamp my legs together to stop the ache if I could, but his huge body is still between them, not allowing me any movement. I'm melting for this man. And it isn't the fact that he's insanely sexy. It's more. It's *him*.

He wraps his arms around me again, pulling me into his chest for another firm squeeze. "Did you know I was here?"

I take a deep breath, confused by his implication. Is he saying that I followed him here? To school?

"What? I didn't know at first…but I, I saw you…" The truth comes rushing back into the front of my mind. Vincent has a girlfriend. Vincent is Borignone mafia. I physically shrink back from him.

His eyes change as if he notices the change in my demeanor and isn't happy about it. "When did you see me?" Lines form on his forehead. Clearly, Vincent isn't a man who is used to surprises.

I shrug, trying my best not to sound as broken as I feel. "I saw you with your g-girlfriend in the dining hall." I wish I were one of those girls who could look him in the eye and dare him to lie to my face. Instead, my voice comes out sounding insecure and small. I drop my eyes to the floor. Even though he's the liar, I'm the one who is embarrassed. He saw me as a girl who wasn't worthy to be his. He made me feel as though we had something special, but clearly, I was mistaken.

He presses his thumb under my chin to lift up my head. "There's a lot to that, Eve. But, I'm just…" he sighs, tracing my full lips with his finger, stunning me quiet with his gentleness. "I just can't believe this. I need to explain everything to you, and I promise I will. But, can we just chill tonight?" He lets out a deep breath as I sit, staring at him in confusion. He wants to hang out tonight? What. The. Hell? I stare at him like he's insane.

"I know you must be hurt by what you've heard." He has the decency to look down for a moment, but when he lifts them back to meet mine, his dark eyes are full of hope. "Can we just pretend that we're all good, and trust that I'll explain it all later? Nothing is as it seems. Trust me."

My rational mind is saying no. Actually, it's screaming "FUCK NO" at the top of its lungs. But my heart is beating with the word "Yes." He's here and I can't believe how much I missed him. I almost forgot how good it felt to be looked at in this way. How could this Vincent I'm staring at be the man in the photos? It just can't be! The man I'm staring at is warm, loving, and gentle. He saved me from the hands of a madman. He doesn't gallivant around town with a socialite and then kill people after hours with the mob! I can't reconcile his sides.

He seems to sense my hesitancy because before I can make a final decision, he steps forward, hugging me into his chest, essentially making the choice for me. He lifts me back into his arms and gently sets me back on my feet. "I may not deserve this chance. But fuck if I'm not gonna take it." His voice is rough, and damn my traitorous body, but it melts a little more for him.

"Wait right at the door. Give me a second, yeah?" I step outside and the door closes. A minute later, I hear the flush of a toilet and the water turn on, as though he's washing his hands. Finally, he exits. The look of relief on his face that I didn't leave is evident.

Taking my hand, his steps are certain and strong as we walk. The crowd of people literally parts as he moves. I'm trailing behind, nervously holding onto his hand, but keeping my head down. We get into the kitchen when he picks me up with something that feels like tenderness, totally at odds with his hard demeanor. He places me on top of the marble counter.

I move my lips to his ear, whispering, "Why do you keep manhandling me?"

"Don't take that away from me," he whispers back, bending his head so we can continue to speak at eye level. "You know I love it. You're so tiny and it feels so good to keep you safe." He moves his gaze from my lips up to my eyes and back down again.

"But, Vincent, I don't need—"

"I know you don't need. But I want."

His dark eyes shine, telling me he sees me. And the truth is, he's the only one who ever has. He licks his full lips. "God, Eve, you look—" he stops. Raking his hands through his hair, seemingly to gather himself. "Are you happy here? Are you living in the dorms? You have everything you need, right?"

Instead of replying, I want to ask him some questions of my own. Like, where the hell has he been? And how could he see me when he had a fucking girlfriend? And how did he hide the fact that he's *Vincent Borignone*? I internally groan, feeling frustrated. Apparently, I talk a big game. But when push comes to shove, I have no backbone. Why the hell am I sitting here in front of him? If I were Janelle, I would have raged and caused a huge scene. I would make sure that he paid the price for lying to me! Better yet, she would have thrown one of these huge bottles of Vodka at his head. But, I'm not Janelle. And when I'm near Vincent, I lose all rational thought.

"Breathe," he says, giving me a crooked grin. "I promise we'll talk about everything, okay? You didn't change your mind now about hanging out, have you?" His voice is full of question and I manage to nod my head, albeit reluctantly.

"Yes. I mean, no, I…I haven't changed my mind." I feel my face turning beet red.

He steps between my legs again, moving his mouth to my ear. "Don't change." He grabs a bottle of water from the counter and drinks it down in a swallow. Dropping the empty bottle in the sink, he leans forward on his hands, caging me in. The party may be full, but we may as well be alone. His face is so close to mine that I can feel the energy coursing between us. Right now, it's no one and nothing other than us. My heart falters as he speaks to me with his eyes. Everything in this moment becomes so simple. I stare at his face, trying to memorize every feature. I can't believe how much I missed him.

Tom throws his arm around Vincent and I gasp from the intrusion. "Wake up, brother. You're at a public party, remember?" Tom laughs, but it seems there's a hard undercurrent to his words. He's looking at Vincent with a face that says *get the fuck away from her*. I turn to Vincent, who is scowling at him.

After their strange standoff, Vincent moves his face back to mine. "This asshole is always pushing me to come out to these fucking parties. Now that I'm here, he's unhappy." He shuffles to the side, shifting an enormous shoulder. For a moment, I remember what he looks like without a shirt on and I feel a throb in my lower belly. Vincent has a body that I'd swear was airbrushed if not for the fact that he's a living, breathing human and not on a billboard in Times Square. He's just so…big. Everywhere. I touch my hand to my face and feel it heating up again.

"Yeah," Tom replies. "You're supposed to come out to chill with your *girlfriend*, right?" He exaggerates the word girlfriend.

My breath gets clogged in my throat; I feel like reality just came over and bitch-slapped me. It's obvious Tom isn't happy that Vincent is talking to me right now. My hands grip the edge of the counter, wanting to jump off and escape when Vincent grabs my thigh with his hand, essentially keeping me frozen to the spot.

"You're a funny guy, Tom. Eve here is my friend. You better treat her with some goddamn respect, brother." He spits out his last word like a curse.

Tom stares at me hard. "Hello, Eve. Welcome to Columbia University." With those words, he steps back to Claire. I blink nervously.

"So, how are your classes going?" Vincent licks the corner of his lips as he leans his side against the counter, ignoring what just happened with Tom. I'm still staring at him dumbly, the stress making my throat immobile. "Ignore him, yeah? I'll deal with him later." I shiver at his words. They're laced with promise, and not the good kind.

I press my lips together. "My classes are actually p-pretty good. I like them."

I may be crazy about the old Vincent, but I'm not equipped to handle this new one. As if he knows I'm wavering, he places his hands above my knees, bringing me back into his orbit. I suck my stomach in and take a sharp breath; his proximity is intoxicating. "There are a few kinds of kids at school. You're obviously the first kind." His words are teasing, but the way his hands are gripping my thighs are anything but.

"Oh?" My voice squeaks. My entire body is burning up from the heat of his hands and how good it feels to be touched—no—gripped by him.

He raises his eyebrows, fastening his hold. "You think I don't know you, Eve?" His heavy hands move slightly higher and my eyes widen. "I know you. I remember every single detail. I know you love the stress and the classes and the assignments. Pop quizzes make you giddy. You're like, 'Hell yeah! I did the reading; I'm gonna ace this test with my huge brain!'" He speaks in a high voice, making fun of me. Meanwhile, his hands keep roaming up inch by inch. I feel like I may pass out.

"Yeah, so what?" I bite the inside of my cheek but can't stop the laugh that's beginning to bubble in my chest. The asshole really does know me! I try to cover my face with my hands, but there's no stopping it. He picks up his hands from my thighs and brings me into his chest to laugh with me. My laughter only intensifies and I try to control myself, the result being a loud snort. He guffaws when he hears it and I want to die of embarrassment.

Moments later he stops, his face turning serious. It's as if yesterday I were in his apartment, sleeping next to him in his bed, feeling like I was finally home.

"Oh, Eve," he says on an exhale. "You're probably carrying your books around like a good little nerd. Tell me you wear a backpack! Wait..." he pauses, moving back from me for a moment. "Are you as good in math as you are in English?" As usual, for Vincent, I always want to rise to the occasion. I nod my head *yes* excitedly, but then die a little inside that I do, in fact, have a backpack. I'm going to go home and throw it into the garbage.

"Is Vincent laughing? Holy shit, but I never thought I'd see the day!" Tom shakes his head in surprise while Claire's mouth hangs open.

"I laugh," Vincent says, his face like stone. "I just never laugh with you because, well, you aren't funny." It's clear Vincent is still angry over Tom's words from a few minutes ago.

"I am funny as hell. Claire, tell him how funny I've been tonight."

"You're hilarious," she deadpans, rolling her eyes as if he is the most unfunny guy she's ever met. Her eyes then move to mine, and they're saying: what the hell is going on here?

Vincent chuckles silently and turns back to me. "Okay, Ms. Brainiac. What's forty-seven times fifteen?"

"Seven hundred five," I reply. He looks at me with surprise but continues.

"One hundred twenty-two times seven plus forty-six?"

I picture the numbers in my head. "Nine hundred. That's easy, give me more." We're both laughing again, and I feel like we're inside this warm and gooey bubble. Everything and everyone outside of us is blurry and dull and… silent.

Wait a second. I look around and realize that the silence is not just in my head. Every single person in the kitchen is staring at us. I hear a voice say, "Who the hell is that?"

Before things can get more awkward, I turn to Claire, relieved that she didn't leave our side. "Vincent, do you know Claire?" He smiles at her and her face immediately falters. He outstretches his hand in a greeting.

"Hey." With only one word, her face changes from white to red. Honestly, it's not her fault. Looking at Vincent straight-on is hard to do without crumbling. Tom rolls his eyes at her inability to speak and throws a possessive arm over her shoulder.

"Tell me something, Claire," Vincent starts. "Seven thousand one hundred fifty divided by thirteen."

"Five hundred fifty. Why?" Her eyes bounce between Vincent and Tom. Claire may be gorgeous, but she's obviously wicked smart.

"Damn, you two girls deserve each other."

Some of Vincent's hair gets into his eyes and I'm yearning to push it off his face. Instead, I look away. *I shouldn't be doing this.*

"Yo, let's play quarters!" Tom grabs a bunch of beers and cups off the counter.

Claire takes my hand and pulls me toward the couch with a face full of question. She glances back and forth between Vincent and me as if she's trying to understand what is going on. I shrug because I don't have any answers.

We drop down onto the *L*-shaped leather couch and the boys sit on the bottom of the *L* so that we can all see each other. Tom explains the rules of the game to me; we each get a chance to bounce a quarter off the table and try to get it into one of the cups full of beer. If you get your quarter into a cup, you choose who in the group has to drink it. The boys keep getting their quarters in and making Claire and me drink. Before I know it, we're drunk in the best possible way. I feel free and relaxed as I laugh at something stupid Tom says. The alcohol has thankfully shut my inner voice up. All I can see and feel in this moment is a blissful buzz and Vincent's warm gaze.

Soon enough, the game is forgotten as Tom begins telling us stories about my economics professor, Ms. Williams. Apparently, she used to dance in a cage at Exit, a huge dance club in the city.

"Yo Vincent, remember the moment you noticed it was your professor dancing up there? Jesus...her tits! I was ready to fuckin' sign up for college after that show!"

"You don't go here?" I ask.

"Nope. Just come out to party with this asshole."

I look back at Vincent and my laughter abruptly stops when I glance down at his pants and confirm that he's carrying a gun. Other people wouldn't notice, but I'm not other people. I was raised in the hood. How the hell did I not realize in the bathroom just now? Or any of the times we were together last year? Vincent muddles my brain.

The conversation is continuing, but I'm not listening anymore. Terror starts to move through my body. His last name isn't just a name; this is Vincent Borignone. My heart thumps so hard I feel sick. He's killed people. He's a thug. Borignone mafia.

He notices the change in me and sits up to move closer. I lean back, not wanting him to come any closer. The look on his face tells me that he knows what I'm thinking; I forgot how easily Vincent is able to read me. My eyes flicker down to his pants, and he slightly nods, letting me know that yes, he's carrying right now.

Shrill laughter breaks me out of my mental fog and seems to be coming from above me. I look up only to see a tall blonde teetering in her heels. It's like slow motion as she falls into me, about to turn me into party roadkill. But before she can crash down, Vincent jumps up, catching her mid-fall. How can a man so big be so agile?

He sets her straight and when she looks at him, she freezes. "Oh, um, hi Vincent." He dismisses her by turning his back and taking a seat next to me.

"You okay?" he whispers centimeters from my ear. I blink for a second longer than necessary, remembering what his lips feel like. Soft and warm, but so demanding. I'm in the midst of emotional whiplash right now.

"Stop eye-fucking my girl," Claire says with a giggle. "I know she's insanely hot, but keep it in the pants, would you?" He jumps away from me as if he's been slapped. Meanwhile, Tom is looking at him angrily.

I turn around, noticing that mostly everyone in the party is gone. I need to get out of here. Before I can say goodbye, Claire stands up.

"Why don't we all go out? The night is still young! Eve has an ID too, right? We can go wherever."

"We?" My eyes open wide.

Vincent laughs at my comment as if it were a joke. "Let's head over to Goldbar. I heard DMX is coming for Shaun Roses' birthday."

I turn to Claire, moving my head side to side in the universal gesture for *no*. Not one to take no for an answer apparently, Claire grabs my hand and pulls me toward the elevator. "Don't back out, Eve. This is once in a lifetime."

"But—"

"No buts. We're gonna end up having the best night ever! Tom and Vincent are probably the most well-connected men in the city, and if you don't go, I can't go. Please come. I'll owe you!" She puts her hands up in prayer and I huff, looking up at the ceiling. I can't say no to her right now. I'm trying to be social. I'm trying to change my life around. Backing out of this would mean ending a brand-new friendship that I'm not ready to lose. I guess I could go and then leave once we get there. I can use the headache excuse.

"Fine," I reply dejectedly.

She jumps up and down excitedly as the guys walk over to us. Vincent cracks his knuckles, a serious look on his face.

We step into the elevator. Vincent is next to me, but I focus on when I'll state my excuse. Should I wait until we're at the bar?

Exiting the building, we wait on the dim corner for a moment when a long black Escalade pulls up to where we're standing. The driver steps out of the car and opens the door for us. Claire goes inside first and Tom jumps in behind her. I walk inside next, my heart leaping from my chest as Vincent sits directly next to me. Claire and Tom are in the third row, behind us, giving us privacy I wish we didn't have. The driver slams the door shut behind us.

The inside of the car is dark. I try to breathe slowly and concentrate on my own heartbeat. When we stop at the next light, I'll use my headache excuse and ask to be taken back to the dorms. That's all. Vincent may be a liar with a girlfriend, but he would never hold me against my will, right? I stuff my hand into my purse and grip my phone. I need something to hold onto; it's like a lifeline right now. I try not to notice that Vincent's huge legs are spread wide on the seat, brushing against mine. I can sense from my side eye that he's turning toward me.

I quickly turn my head and look up. "Vincent—"

"Shhh," he replies, moving closer to me so our legs are flush. "Tonight, let's have fun. I'll explain everything later. Trust me, Eve." He puts his hands up, tucking some loose strands of hair behind my ear with so much intimacy, my heart squeezes.

Right on the heels of that feeling, indignation runs through my blood. How dare he touch me after what I've learned?

"What are you doing? Back off!" I whisper-yell. Maybe it's the darkness, but my outrage and resentment are finally coming through. I didn't sacrifice everything only to get sucked back into this life.

He sighs, physically moving back from me. "Let's just be us tonight. I want you to give me that."

"No," I huff. "I changed my mind. I can't do this. Take me home." I cross my hands over my chest, trying to protect myself.

"Come on. Just one night." His voice is tight; it's obvious he isn't accustomed to pleading. "DMX is playing. How can you say no to that?" His white teeth shine and I immediately want to knock them out.

"Vincent Borignone." I state his full name like a curse. "You're a liar! And I want to go home," I hiss.

"Don't say that. I told you I'd explain." He's angry now, sitting taller than a moment ago.

"What could you possibly say?" My words come out with fury. We both look behind us and see that Claire and Tom are making out in the back, seemingly oblivious to what's going on right in front of them.

Vincent straightens. "Can you turn up the volume, please?" he asks the driver.

"Yes, sir." Britney Spears' "I'm a Slave For You" gets louder.

"Tonight, let everything go. I swear to God. I swear to Jesus. I'll explain everything to you later, okay? Don't go back on your word. You should trust me, after everything I've done for you."

"You're kidding, right? How dare you throw our past in my face?"

His entire demeanor sets in a hard line. This man isn't going to play fair and it's clear he isn't above using everything in his arsenal to get what he wants. He's right, though. He saved my life. I owe him.

"Fine." I angle my body toward the window. I may go out with him tonight, but that doesn't mean I have to enjoy it.

CHAPTER 4

VINCENT

She pulls the tie out of her hair and her hair falls in waves, draping around her small shoulders. I'm immediately assaulted by a sweet coconut scent blended with something uniquely Eve.

"Your hair…it got even longer. I love it like this." Even though I know that Tom and Claire aren't listening to us, I'll use their existence as an excuse to get closer. I watch her take a sharp breath as I bring my hand to her hair, gently pushing it aside to see her beautiful neck.

She stares out the window, the softness of her profile melting my insides. Her nose is small and slightly turned up, lips full, hair dark and natural…everything about her, on a physical level, works for me. I know I don't deserve it, but if she's willing to say yes, I'm not going to turn it away just because I had to bring up some hard shit to get her to agree. I'll explain everything to her later, but before I do, I need to remind her how good we are together.

I'm waiting for her to look back at me, but she doesn't. I'm not a patient man, and I have zero tolerance for being ignored.

"Eve." My voice comes out harshly, but it works. She finally moves her head, and everything is written clearly on her face; I have no choice but to pause. Does she know how obvious her love is? How pure? It takes my goddamn breath away and makes me curse who I am and where I come from. How can I see a woman like this, after all she's been through, and bring her back into my world of violence? Would she ever accept my life?

I always loved women. Being with Daniela had zero bearing on my extracurricular activities. I live in New York City, not some small town in Nebraska; there's no shortage of pussy here. But Eve was never the kind of girl who would just be a regular fuck. I knew it the moment I first laid eyes on her. I had only just met her and immediately brought her to one of my restaurants. I think there was a part of me that was always looking for her. And the moment our eyes met, everything clicked in place.

The vehicle stops and the driver jumps out, opening our door. We all exit the car and immediately walk to the front of the long line, my huge hand holding her tiny one as we step forward. She squeezes my palm nervously and I look down at her. "I've got you." She looks at me and slightly nods, seemingly reassured. She believes she's safe with me. Again, I ask myself, what the fuck am I doing?

"Vincent, what up man?"

I fist bump the enormous bouncer who I'd guess weighs over two-fifty. He moves to the side as he opens the red-velvet rope. I turn to Eve as we step into the club, noticing the wide-eyed look on her face as if she's never seen something so beautiful. Just like its name, the entire bar is gold. The walls are lined with golden skulls and even the drapes are gold. Giant crystal chandeliers hang from the ceiling, giving the place a warm glow.

We're ushered to a private table in the back with a perfect view of the dance floor. Eve and I sit together on one side, Claire and Tom on the other.

Eve is watching raptly as half-naked bodies gyrate to the music in front of us; I take her hand, rubbing my thumb across her knuckles.

The table server saunters over to us in a tiny bikini top and shorts, her tits and ass pouring out of both. She bends down seductively, placing a large golden bucket on our table filled with bottles of vodka and glass jugs of cranberry and orange juice. She pauses before walking away, her eyes flaring with interest. Once upon a time, I'd take this woman up on her offer. We both know that with a nod, I could get this woman on her knees in the club's back room. The entire thing—like almost everything in life—is a transaction. She wants my dick, and I feel horny. One plus one equals two. Crazy how over the last twelve months, just the idea of a woman other than the beauty next to me is enough to turn my stomach.

"Can I get you something?" She slowly scrapes a long fingernail against the back of my neck. I grab her wrist, probably harder than necessary, turning my head so I'm staring at her hard.

"Don't touch me." Her eyes widen in fear. Finally, when I'm good and ready, I let her go. She scurries away.

I turn to Eve then, but her eyes are still trained on the dance floor. I'm glad she didn't catch that exchange with the waitress; most of these women are disrespectful as fuck. They don't deserve to breathe the same air as my girl. Dropping a hand on her leg and gently caressing her thigh, she turns to me, biting her lip, as if she's conflicted. She probably doesn't want to enjoy herself, but the music is amazing and the crowd is hot.

Still, this girl, she fills me up inside exactly how I need. Yeah, she's seen some bad shit. But somehow, she's maintained this… *innocence*. She may be better than a man like me deserves, but now that I've got her, there's no way I'm letting her go again. I want to do right by her, but I'm not a fuckin' saint.

She inches closer to me. "So, DMX, huh?" Her face is so expectant I have to hold myself back from not throwing my arms around her and mauling her right here at the table. I shift my body, adjusting my dick in my jeans. She has no idea how special she is. Other girls would be sitting on my lap, trying to do whatever they could to keep my interest. They'd be asking me what they could do for me. They'd beg to meet DMX. But Eve isn't other girls.

Instead of saying all of these things, I reply with one word: "Yes."

"Vincent..." she takes a deep breath, looking as if she's ready to go off on a rant. I stop her with a hand on her thigh.

"Shut that brain of yours off tonight. A promise is a promise, Eve." I move to the edge of the couch and pour three shot glasses of vodka. I hand one glass to her and pick the other two up for myself.

"Are you asking me not to think, Vincent? Because any time a man asks a woman not to think—"

"I'm not asking you. I'm telling you." I can't take my eyes off her. I go ahead and throw back one drink, waiting patiently for her to take hers. "I dare you, Eve," I say with a joking smile, trying to bring the moment down a notch. It isn't easy for me to be playful, but I want to be.

She purses her lips, doing her best not to laugh. "Listen. If I take this drink, it's not because you're daring me." She raises an eyebrow.

"No?" She wants to play? I'll play.

"No." Her lips slightly pucker at the end of the word, and I can't help but stare at them. "It's because I'm in college now, and I can drink if I want to. Understand?" Her attitude and this newfound strength only turns me on more.

"By all means, college girl. Be free to experiment." I pause. "But only with me, when I can make sure you're safe."

"I can take care of myself, Vincent. I've been through a lot, in case you've forgotten."

"I haven't forgotten anything. Not even a minor detail." I pause, looking her up and down until her face heats. "But getting drunk in a place where someone can easily spike your drink? That's not experimenting. That's just stupid."

She clears her throat. "So, right now, you're giving me this drink because?" She cocks that gorgeous head of hers to the side, waiting for my response.

"Because I want you to relax and let go a bit. Have some of that college fun you deserve. *Safely*."

She lifts the glass to her pouty lips, swallowing the drink. Her face scrunches from the burn and I hand her a lemon. She takes a bite and breathes a sigh of relief.

"L-listen, Vincent." Her earlier bravado turns to hesitation. "I know you took care of some stuff for me in the past. But I'm not that girl anymore, okay? I'm not looking for someone to run my life. And I sure as hell am not trying to get wrapped up in your… family business. I spent close to nineteen years running away from that shit, and I'm not getting brought back into it—"

"—And I'm not looking to drag you into something you don't want. I helped you out, as a friend. You don't owe me anything, understand? I brought it up in the car because I wanted you to come out with me tonight. I felt like seeing you. Not because I wanted compensation."

She nods, letting out a relieved exhale. A better man may feel guilty for lying, but not me. Killing Carlos was never for the sake of friendship. Every punch and kick—until he was writhing in his own blood on the floor—every ounce of heat I gave that fucker with my fists, was payback. He thought he could torment my woman, nearly rape her, and get away with it? I made him pay like the dirty snake he was. I'm still the son of Antonio Borignone. And no one fucks with me and mine.

She lifts her face. "Can we have some fun now?"

Tom drops next to me, growling in my ear. "This bitch has you by the fucking balls, Borignone. Stop this shit!" He's seething.

I want to grab his throat, tell him if he ever speaks to me like that again, I'll put a bullet in his head. But Eve is next to me looking so happy, and there's no way I'd jeopardize that. I swallow down my anger, focusing on her instead.

Standing, I bring her with me to the center of the dance floor. She's got great rhythm, so obviously comfortable in her own skin when she's dancing. It's at odds with her regular shyness. I can tell she's holding back for now, and I can't wait until she lets go.

I maintain a slight distance, which is difficult for me; I always take what I want. But with Eve, I've always held back. The arrogant prick inside me knows that with her, everything needs to be different. I've gotta shut up and wait.

Song after song comes and goes, and we don't stop moving. It's Eminem. We're still not close enough, but I can see her body relaxing. We're in our own orbit; I'm going to keep us here for as long as I can.

The song changes again and then again. It's "In Da Club" by 50 Cent. His gravel voice blares from the speakers and the entire dance floor cheers. We're sweating, and her cheeks are flushing pink. My eyes rove around her small and curvy body. She's wearing a simple cotton tank top with a white lacy bra underneath, but holy shit if it's not sexier than all of these girls who are walking around half nude. Her hair is down and free, the way I love it.

She finally takes a step closer, letting me know I don't have to keep a distance. I bring my arms around her and we immediately fall into step. How is it possible I can connect with someone in this way? My arms move to her small waist and she turns her body so her back is against my front. She's sweating, and it makes her scent more acute. My dick hardens. Eve may have been a book nerd for her entire life, but it's obvious she was made to dance. I stay with her, keeping control of our movements but at the same time giving her room to do her own thing.

She turns. "Vincent, I want another drink," she yells happily over the music.

I pull her back through the crowd to get to the table, immediately pouring three more shots. I hand her another drink, taking the other two for myself.

She's about to grab it from my hands when I pull it back. "You don't have to finish this, okay? Just a sip."

Smirking at me in defiance, she lifts it up and swallows the whole thing down. I shake my head as I give her a slice of lemon, watching her teeth sink into the bitterness. She lifts her shoulders, daring me to stop her. I can only laugh as I quickly shoot down my own drinks. I've been drinking alcohol for so many years now, it would take another five to get me drunk.

We're back on the dance floor when she starts giggling, leaning on me. She may think she doesn't need anyone, but why fight through life alone when you can have back up?

DMX gives the crowd his signature growl, and the entire room instantly starts screaming with excitement. I feel someone push against me. I open my eyes to look around, noticing the dance floor is completely full. I wrap my arms around Eve's shoulders protectively, making sure she's safe and comfortable. Somehow, we've landed ourselves in a mosh pit.

She's jumping up and down in excitement. I chuckle at her exuberance. Some guys bump into us and I turn my head quickly, glaring. They move to the side, but within a few minutes, the crowd grows aggressive. Eve won't feel comfortable in this.

She starts to lose her footing as people continue to push forward, trying to get closer to the stage. She looks at me with an anxiety-filled face and I immediately walk us off the packed floor.

The moment we get to the table, she starts in a rush. "I'm sorry. I couldn't. It was too much—"

I push an errant hair from her face and she quiets. "Don't ever apologize." I turn to Tom while Eve hangs on my side. He's staring at us, an angry look on his face. "Yo, Tom. We're out." He stands up to shake my hand goodbye; I squeeze his as hard as I can, letting him know without words that he and I have shit to discuss later. I know he's only thinking of the best for me, but if he ever disrespects my girl again, I'll make him pay.

Eve and I walk out of the club. The cool air feels good. I'm about to take out my phone to call the driver when Eve, seemingly out of the blue, says, "I'm lost." She lifts her hand to her lips, surprised that she said that out loud.

I turn to her. "No, baby. I found you, remember?" She stares up at me, all purity and trust. I need to get us out of here.

I pull out my phone from my jacket pocket and type to the driver to come get us. Her eyes are trained on my face; she's studying me. Never in my life have I given a fuck about my looks. I know women like what they see, but my face was never something I had to work for and therefore, it's not something I'm particularly proud of. But the way Eve is looking at me now—memorizing every feature of my face—makes me want to give God a high five.

"Your mom was Native American, right? You look it." She blushes. She's drunk, staring at me with wide eyes like I created the damn universe in four days. I do my best to resist the urge to lift her into my arms.

I put my phone away and pull my jacket off, draping it around her tiny shoulders. It hangs on her, falling to the middle of her calves.

"Tell me you have a coat." I pull the sides of my jacket around her so that the wind won't get through. It's not too cold, but she definitely isn't dressed warmly enough for a fall New York City night.

"Yeah, I do. I just bought a new coat from Barneys yesterday at the bargain price of five hundred dollars," she deadpans.

I chuckle. "Five hundred? Is that it?" She pulls my jacket closer to her body, smelling the collar and tightly shutting her eyes.

The black Escalade pulls up. As the driver moves to get out of the car, I shake my head, letting him know to stay put. Eve is mine tonight, and I want to be the one to hold the door for her. I open it and she climbs inside first. Taking a look at her perfect heart-shaped ass, I groan at all the things I wish I could do. I follow in behind her and shut the door as I sit inside. Without another word, the car heads downtown.

"Are we going to your SoHo apartment?" She clasps her hands together nervously. The last time I brought her to my place downtown, she opened up to me about Carlos. Hopefully tonight, I'll be able to have another honest conversation with her.

Moving my hands around her waist, I pull her to sit on my lap. She leans her head in the crook of my neck and shoulder as if it were the most natural thing in the world. When her eyes shut, I feel relief like I've never known. How can she fit so well in my arms? I ask myself for the hundredth time, what the fuck am I doing? Normally, I'm calculated. I don't do shit without thinking it all through. Consequences. Positive outcomes. Potential disasters. I'm a numbers and logic man. And this? This is something I never do: *emotion.*

We get to my building. The doorman holds the door and I strut through, Eve following right behind me. I still haven't said a word to her since we got into the car. Standing together in the elevator, she barely reaches the center of my chest. She's biting her lip, and fuck if I don't want to throw her against the wall right now.

We step off and walk to my door, where I type my security codes. Before pushing the door open, I pause to take a look at Eve and wonder if I'm not about to make an enormous mistake. She stares at me with absolute trust, and I know that I can't stop myself. I want this woman.

CHAPTER 5

EVE

I want to act like he's the same Vincent I used to know, but he isn't. The Vincent I used to know wasn't this dangerous looking, was he? I look down at his pants again, noticing the outline of his gun. God, help me. How can I be so afraid, but so turned on at the same time?

We get inside and I try not to let my jaw drop at his perfect apartment. It's just as beautiful as I remember. We step into his open kitchen area, and he leaves his keys on the marble countertop. Grabbing two cold bottles of water from the fridge, he opens the cap before handing me one. I take a deep pull, letting the cold water wet my dry throat.

He said we'd discuss everything. Is that why he brought me here? To tell me about Daniela? I can't handle it. I don't think I'd survive if he told me he loves her. If he told me that I was a mistake. If he told me he never meant to hurt me, or some other bullshit. It's bad enough to hear about Daniela through the gossip mill and it's even worse to see them together. But to hear about their relationship from Vincent's perfect lips? It would break me. I'd rather just pretend we aren't at school together; move on and let what we had be a good memory. He can continue being the hot guy on campus, and I can keep my head in the books.

We stare at each other, time seemingly suspended. I'm desperate for him not to tell me more than I already know. How can I stop this conversation from happening? I notice his pupils starting to dilate and the quickening of his breath.

At once, we both step toward each other. I look up into his face when he lifts me in his arms. Before I change my mind, I press my lips against his. He pulls away, his eyes searching mine. I slightly nod my head. He starts by slowly kissing every piece of my lips as if I'm something to be savored.

When his tongue finally enters my mouth, I grab a fistful of his hair and moan. It must register with him how badly I want this because with that sound he finally starts to kiss me like his life depends on it. He consumes me with his mouth, moving to my neck as he nudges my legs wider to make room for his hips.

"You're shaking," he tells me between kisses. I feel out of my mind.

I'm hot. Cold. Soaked.

He moves his hands down my legs, pulling the shoes off my feet. They clatter like dead weights onto the wooden floor. I'm trembling like it's twenty below. He presses my body against the wall while he pulls his shirt over his head with one arm. My heart hammers. His body heat is off the charts. My hands move on their own accord up to his massive shoulders and down along his sides. I pull in a hard breath as I trace the gorgeous V-shape of his back.

"Get this off," he demands, tugging at my shirt.

I try to get myself out of my tank top, but it gets stuck on my arm. "There we go," he says as he untangles the fabric and lifts it up. I groan in relief, grabbing his hair with my hands and pulling him to my mouth again. I can't help myself.

He hums, and I feel the vibration straight into my core. His fingers graze over my nipples, up and down, until they're hardened peaks. My bra is on, but the cotton is so thin I can feel the roughness of the calluses against my sensitive skin. I want to tear my clothes off. I want direct contact. My lower belly clenches in anticipation.

He finally unhooks my bra, roughly pulling it off my shoulders and stopping with a hiss, taking me in with his hooded eyes. "My memory doesn't do you justice. Jesus Christ, Eve. You're fucking perfect. Perfect." His mouth lowers over my bare nipple and with his first hard suck, tremors instantly wrack my body. "Ahhhh!"

"Always so responsive to me." He moves his mouth to my other breast and I try to contain the pleasure. It's almost too much. I bite the side of my cheek, wanting to stay quiet.

"Moan for me, baby. I need to hear you. No one here but us." As if I have a choice! I'm gripping the back of his shoulders as the fire inside me rages.

He lifts his mouth, letting his thumbs graze against my neck. "Tell me, Eve, has anyone other than me touched you?" I can't manage a reply; it all feels too good.

He stops moving. "Answer me."

"N-no."

He moves his nose into my neck, scenting me as he pushes his hardness into my core. "You're mine, do you understand?"

"Vincent!" I cry, screwing my eyes shut.

JESSICA RUBEN

CHAPTER 6

VINCENT

With the moan of my name from her lips, I'm brought back to reality. I pull my mouth away. *You can't do this*, my mind echoes. I stare at her face, flushed from her high cheekbones down to her perfect cherry nipples. I want this so bad, but I need to control myself. It takes her a few seconds to realize that I've stopped. At first, her eyes open wide with so much joy…

And then she blinks.

The realization that something is wrong moves through her face. She must see remorse is written all over me because her smile falls.

"Eve," I pant, dropping my head into her neck, trying to slow myself down. She places her small hands behind my head, holding me close. She's comforting me when she should be slapping me across the face.

"W-what happened?" She looks at me openly, her eyes and body so full of tenderness that it makes my knees weak. I touch her face, smoothing out the stress lines on her forehead. I'm angry that she'll allow me to do this to her when she deserves so much more. I haven't even explained things yet!

"I'm not going to fuck you like this, here against the wall." My voice comes out harsher than I intended. I sigh, telling myself to calm down. "That's not who you are."

I set her down on the floor and she immediately bends down, picking up her crumpled clothes. Her dark hair is wild, draped around her shoulders and covering the tops of her breasts. She slides her shivering arms into her threadbare bra, hands moving to her back to shut the clasp. This is my fault.

I step behind her, gently hooking her bra together. Her body trembles, literally shakes like a leaf, while I put her shirt back on, adjusting her straps so they aren't tangled.

I need to talk to her. We need to be open and she needs to know what's going on. The time for withholding truth is over. If she and I have any hope for the future, we have to go about this the right way, with honesty.

"There are obviously things I didn't tell you. I need to start by saying that I shouldn't have given you those drinks. Tonight was entirely my fault. I was hoping for a little more time with you before I had to bring all of this shit up." I shut my mouth tightly, breathing through my nose.

Her head is down as if she's embarrassed by her behavior. Doesn't she realize that this isn't one-sided?

"Eve, don't put your head down." I take her hand, bringing her to my couch. I maneuver us so that the height difference isn't as pronounced. I want her to feel like an equal.

"You're Vincent Borignone," she says, biting the side of her quivering lip. "I need to get out of here." She makes a move to turn away, but I hold her in place. I move my thumb to her cheek, brushing the tears off with the pads of my thumbs. Her huge brown eyes have turned into a honey hazel blend. "How could I do that, Vincent? How could I, and how could you?" She starts to cry in earnest and I bring her closer to me.

"Don't cry, baby. I swear to you, I understand. What we have is difficult to control. What happened tonight was my fault, all right? Blame me."

"And you're…you've got a—"

"You heard things, right? About me? And Daniela, too. What do you think you know? Tell me everything, Eve, and we'll sort it out together. The time for secrets is behind us now." I'm waiting for her to break down and tell me everything she knows. And then I want to wrap her up in my arms and tell her the entire dirty truth.

She sniffles, trying to catch her breath. "You have a g-girlfriend. Your father is Antonio. You're B-Borignone mafia."

"The internet, and Daniela, in particular, have a way of molding reality. She is very talented at giving just enough honesty in her photography that the lies become camouflaged."

"Vincent—I don't want to know, okay? I've learned enough through the gossip mill and the internet."

"So, you used to hide behind your sister and your books, and you're trying to continue that? Eve, you can't live in darkness. If we're going to figure this shit out between us, you need to open your eyes—"

"Figure shit out between us? There is no *us*, Vincent."

This girl is mine. She can deny it all she wants, but I know what we have. "You think I'm letting you go again?"

"And what is that supposed to mean? You. Don't. Have. Me." She punctuates every word, but I hear the pain in her undertone.

"We're both here at school together. I'll never be okay with us pretending like the other doesn't exist."

"I don't want to hear it!" Her chest rises and falls with her heavy breathing. "I don't want to learn about how you treated me like I was y-your whore."

Her tears keep falling, but she doesn't stop. "I can't find out more about it because then, everything I believed we had would feel like a lie. I thought we had something; when really, I was nothing to you! You knew me, but I didn't know you. Did you see my mother and think, 'well, she's just like her?'"

"No—"

"You had a girlfriend the entire time! You turned me into a cheater, Vincent! I can't find out more. If you care about me at all, you'll just leave it as a good memory, and move on." She is slashing herself with her words, but I'm the one who sharpened the knife. I need to find a way to dull the edge.

I move closer to her, opening my hands in front of my chest. "Eve. I swear to all that is holy that I never saw you that way. Look into my eyes and trust me. Let me just explain—"

My words come too late; her pain is obviously spiraling. "I can't believe how stupid I was! And you let me be the idiot. I can just imagine, rich and gorgeous Vincent Borignone. Standing in my shitty stairwell with the lights flickering..." She lets out a sardonic laugh. "I've seen countless men do this to my mother. But you would know that already, wouldn't you? She does work as a stripper in one of your—"

I lift my hand, stopping her. "No. You don't deserve to feel like I treated you like trash. I won't allow you to think poorly about what we had." The thought of never touching her again turns my chest hollow. But I calm myself, needing to continue. "I will not let you believe that your first experiences with a man, with me, were tainted. What we had wasn't a damn lie!"

She looks at me, fury surrounding her. "You won't *allow* me?"

I grit my teeth. "I will not." I wait, letting it sink in that there's no way I'm going to walk away from this. From us. "I see how you may think Daniela and I are together on social media. And yeah, we used to fuck." She winces, but I don't let it stop me from speaking the truth. "But things are complicated with us. If you'd just let me—"

I move forward, trying to touch her again. But the way she's staring at my eyes makes it clear that she wants nothing to do with me right now. Eve stands up off the couch, backing away. Even though every part of me is telling me to grab her and force her to listen, I don't want to hurt her any more than I already have. Maybe she needs a few days to process. She got a little drunk tonight, and I want her to be straight when she hears me out.

She turns her angelic face toward the ceiling, trying to look anywhere but at me. "I get it," she hiccups, still refusing my eyes. "You're the king and queen of New York and all that, right? How could you throw something like that away for someone like me?"

"No one is the king and queen of shit," I yell. "Like I said before, it's a lot more complicated than that. It's family business." I try to soften my voice at the end, but nothing is working. I'm not used to feeling so out of control; I hate it.

"Oh, that's great!" she replies sarcastically. "Family business. Let's add that to the list, huh? You're Vincent Borignone, a member of the hardest mafia on the East Coast! You think I don't know what *family business* means?"

"Maybe I'm an associate?"

"Don't give me that bullshit, Vincent. I see how strong and powerful and smart you are! You belong to the family, and they aren't dumb. They probably see you as their golden ticket! And as the son of Antonio—"

"Well, let's start with this," I tell her firmly. "You're right. I'm not just a member. The entire family operation? It's going to be mine one day. All the illegal shit we do? The drugs, the guns? I am my father's right hand." My chest heaves. "And you want to know something crazy? Ever since I met you, I knew I needed and wanted to make a serious change in my life!" I step closer to her, feeling the emotion run through me. "Because of you, I've been in the process of trying to change everything." I yell, my voice echoing around the room.

Instead of backing down, she rises up to me. "Why is it so important to you for me to know the truth? Why do you even care? Let's just stay away from each other. Let the past stay in the past where it belongs."

"Why?" I grumble, my teeth clenched. "Because I fucking lo— " I stop myself, exhaling. "You call to me on a hundred different levels. Because who you are has meaning in my life." I pause, gripping the ends of my hair. "When I thought I'd never see you anymore, the memory of you still mattered. What you stand for matters. Do you understand?" I point to my own chest. "The idea of you walking away from me. Ignoring me. Falsely believing that I took advantage of you last year. I won't have it. This apartment? It's mine and mine alone. No one other than my father, Tom, and my driver knows that it exists. You're the only other person I've ever brought here. You're the only woman who has ever put her head on that pillow. You aren't a side piece. Since the day I met you, you have been the *only* fucking piece!"

I look down at the ground for a moment, clenching my fists. "You've risked your life to get out of that shitty fucking universe you lived in. And I swore to myself then that I'd stay away from you because I didn't want to bring you back down the rabbit hole. But then tonight," I sigh, dropping my head in my hands for a moment. "You showed up. If you think I'm giving up on us now, you're wrong. I let go of you once, and I'm not making that same mistake again."

She opens and closes her mouth a few times, but she doesn't speak.

My phone pings with a text. I lift it from the side table. It's a 9-1-1 from Jimmy. "Fuck!" I roar. "I gotta take you home." I press my lips into a firm line. I've got no choice but to answer this. If a brother needs me, I'm there.

She moves to put on her shoes and I walk into my bedroom, pulling out one of my dark hoodies. It'll probably fall to her knees, but it'll keep her warmer than that thin tank she's got on. When I get into the living room, she's sitting on the couch with her knees up to her chin. I bend over to slide it over her head, pulling her hair through the hood while she threads her arms inside. I realize that she's in somewhat of a shock right now, and I immediately feel like shit. I want to protect her, not hurt her. What have I done?

We get downstairs and my car is waiting for us. She's silent. This time, I don't press my leg against hers. Our conversation will have to wait a few days until she processes what she's learned tonight. I need time with her, without any distractions.

The car pulls up in front of the freshman quad and I put my hand on the door, stopping her from leaving. There's a lot I want to say, but my head is too full. I watch as she shuts her eyes tightly, a lone tear sliding down her beautiful face.

I finally move my hand off the door. She steps out and walks to her dorm, not looking back. I slam my hand on the passenger seat. "Fuck!" I yell. "Take me to Jimmy's," I order the driver.

"Yes, Mr. Borignone."

JESSICA RUBEN

CHAPTER 7

EVE

I cry myself to sleep, fisting my navy sheets. I feel like I'm melting from the heat, but I refuse to take his sweatshirt off. It smells like him—and even though part of me wants to shred the sweatshirt with my bare hands and burn it—just the thought of removing it from my body makes me cry even harder.

In my heart, I know Vincent has good intentions. He wants to make sure I understand what happened. He doesn't ever want me to believe falsehood. But what if he tells me he was fucking her the entire time he saw me? How am I supposed to know he isn't going to tell me something equally as horrible? I spent a year wishing he'd be open and honest, and now all I want to do is beg him to keep his mouth shut.

Finally, my body drifts into a restless sleep.

Sometime later, I hear a hard knock at my door. At first, I hear it in my dreams, but after a few bangs, I spring out of bed. Squinting at the clock, it's one o'clock in the afternoon. I stumble to my door and open it, rubbing the sleep from my eyes.

"Eve? I've been calling your phone all morning. Thank God you're here and not at Vincent's!"

Claire barges into my bedroom, shutting the door behind us. "Vincent." Her eyes practically bug out of her head. "Eve. You and Vincent!" She's practically bouncing on the soles of her feet, actively waiting for a reply.

"What are you staring at me like that for? I just woke up and I've been here all night, okay? Calm down."

"Well, if I didn't know better, I'd say that man wants you. Badly. He couldn't take his eyes off you all night! By the way, DMX was sick! But whatever. Wash up. Let's go out to eat and talk!" She looks me up and down, noticing the large black sweatshirt I'm wearing. I ignore her stare. For all she knows, it's my brother's.

She makes herself at home in the chair by my desk and pulls out a book from her enormous purse. I stare at her in confusion, but she isn't minding me. After a moment, she lifts her head. "Move it, Eve, and get your ass to the bathroom. I'm staaaarving."

I let myself out of the room, too emotionally exhausted to argue.

Under the shower spray, my mind plays back last night's events. Vincent. Vincent. Vincent. His lips. His hands. Dancing. Our fight. His half admission of love. What am I going to do? He wants to talk. He wants to tell me everything so there won't be any more secrets. Is he going to tell me about the family business with Daniela? And do I even want to know the truth? I've spent my life trying to stay away from that bullshit. How is this happening to me?

I walk back into the room physically refreshed, but still unsure what I'm supposed to tell Claire. I change on autopilot, lost in my own head.

She's so engrossed in her book that she barely registers I'm ready to go. I glance at the cover of the paperback she's reading and my eyes widen in surprise. It's a hot guy with a naked torso, covered in tattoos.

"What are you reading?" I ask, suppressing a chuckle.

She slams her book shut, turning red. "Um, nothing…"

"Tell me you're reading porn right now." I bite the side of my cheek, doing my best not to burst into laughter.

"It's not porn! It's really good actually!" I move closer to read the cover when she hides the book behind her back. "It's about this guy in a motorcycle club…and…this girl, well, she was a stripper at first, but then—" She stops talking and we burst into hysterics.

We leave the room to head over to the dining hall on campus. We both need coffee and greasy food badly. Taking a small booth in the back, my stomach growls louder than I thought possible. Claire tells me she'll get the food and I should grab the coffee in order to save time.

The cashier gives me a face when she takes my dining card for the two coffees as if she's annoyed to be helping some hungover rich kid whose daddy makes sure she has enough money in her account each month. I want to tell her that I'm not like that at all; I'm here on full scholarship and the school pays for my food—I'm not some rich asshole. Instead, I just thank her as graciously as I can manage, and walk back to our booth, holding both our mugs of coffee.

Claire sits down right after me, setting a green tray in front of us. Relief settles in my stomach as I unwrap a gigantic egg-and-cheese sandwich, immediately taking a huge bite. While I'm chewing, I pour a small packet of creamer into my coffee mug and watch the color turn from black to light brown. I put the cup to my lips and hum. "Ah, coffee."

"Okay, Eve. I'm ready. Tell me everything." Claire's eyes are shining with excitement as she scoots forward in her seat. Even though I'm a private person, I feel like I can trust her with at least a general outline of events. And the truth is, I'm relieved to have a friend to share this with. Everything has gotten so complicated, and I want support. I know that I need to come clean with Janelle, too.

I clear my throat. "Well, me and Vincent met one night in the Meatpacking District last year. And we ended up going out a few times."

Her eyes widen in shock with my admission. I could have told her I had dinner with the President and she probably wouldn't be as shocked. "Wait. Vincent Borignone took you out? Like, on dates?"

"Um, I guess so?" I stop and look around, making sure no one is eavesdropping. Luckily, everyone around us seems to be busy in their own conversations. "I asked him once what we were doing, but he just said we're *friends*." I shrug. "Look, we have this weird connection. He's gorgeous, but with him, it's more than that. I had no clue that he went to school here! And I definitely didn't know he had a girlfriend."

She breathes in deeply, sucking her bottom lip into her mouth. "Look, Eve. There's a lot I need to tell you because clearly, you don't have a clue. You've looked him up though, right?" She lifts the salt, shaking it over her eggs.

"Yeah." I nod. "I finally did, after lunch that day when I met the girls in Phi Alpha."

"Ah. That's why you ran out." She nods in understanding.

"Listen, we all talk about Vincent all the time because of how hot he is. And yes, there are rumors about his mafia connections. But Eve"—she lowers her voice and moves closer to me—"I don't think they're just rumors. They say he's the son of the biggest mobster in Manhattan! And there must be a grain of truth to that, right? I mean, otherwise, why would that rumor even start? And honestly, look at him! He's scary as fuck! And, Daniela, she's been with him since her freshman year. I guess that's three years now—and to my knowledge, they've never been on a break. I mean, have you seen her social media accounts? Millions of followers!" She's rushing to get the words out.

I feel the need to defend myself. "I didn't even know his last name until lunch! How would I have known he had a girlfriend?"

She lets out a breath but continues. "You know that she's a socialite, right? Her father owns a huge bank in Central America. They're billionaires. Her parents had a Debutant Ball for her at the University Club when she turned eighteen, and people said it was insane! They're not just a college golden couple. They're like, a global golden couple." Her green eyes turn to gray as my face drops. It's obvious that she isn't enjoying this.

"I'm telling you this because you need to know that they aren't"—she takes a breath, thinking of the right word—"*ordinary*. And it's obvious you and Vincent were into each other last night, but trust me, her claws are in him deep. And if Daniela ever found out about whatever went on last year between you guys, let's just say your life would be made into a living hell. She'd make sure you were blackballed from all of Greek life and probably every restaurant and club in New York City. Maybe even beyond that."

My throat tightens. I'm shaking from the anxiety of what I may have gotten myself into. Vincent knows I'm here and he isn't going to stop until he talks to me. He's nothing if not persistent.

"I'll take last night and our conversation to the grave, okay? Don't worry." Looking into her face, I see her honesty.

"But, I really didn't know—"

"I know. Let's change the subject now, yeah? Just promise me you'll stay away from him. Seriously, nothing good can come of it."

I nod my head in agreement, and we spend the rest of our breakfast discussing classes and how to get the best outlines. Apparently, Phi Alpha has an entire room dedicated to notes and exams from almost every professor at school.

When we're done eating, I hug Claire goodbye and get back to my room to crack open my books.

Around eleven o'clock that night, I get a call from Janelle. "Hey, love. How's it going?"

I let out a sigh and move to my bed, swallowing back the tears that are resurfacing in my throat. "I don't know. Something's come up and..." My heart starts to pound. "There's a lot I need to tell you."

"Okay. Now or in person?" Her voice is full of anxiety.

"In person."

"We'll do that. How have classes been this week? I hate hearing you sound miserable. Things were so good the last time we spoke."

I sniffle. "I actually made a new friend and she's pretty cool. Her name is Claire. But she's in this sorority and most of the girls seem like bitches. I'm not used to this…"

"Just take it easy," she says soothingly. "It's okay to have harder days. Nothing is ever simple. But this is what you've been waiting for. Just take it day by day and keep your eye on the prize. Your life isn't just a wish anymore. It's happening. Remember that, okay?" I feel the tears welling up heavily in my eyes, and I know if I open my mouth again, the dam will burst. The last thing I want is for her to worry, so I keep my mouth shut.

"Have you spoken to Ms. Levine? I bet she can help you with what you're feeling. She told me that you'd probably go through something like this at some point." I drop my head and breathe in and out, and the tears start to drop. I want to tell her about Vincent. No, I need to tell her. I can't keep it in anymore. But it can't be over the phone.

"Janelle, are you free tomorrow night for dinner?"

"Yes. And don't cry, Eve, okay? We'll be together and everything will be all right." I hear the kindness in her voice, and it makes my heart squeeze. She's always got my back.

"O-kay," I manage to stutter out.

"Cool. I'll be at your dorm at five. Let's also stop at Bed Bath, get some shit to make your room more like a home. That's bound to help, right? Go to sleep now. Everything will look better in the morning." She hangs up, and I curl into my bed and stare at the wall, images of Daniela and Vincent shifting in front of my eyes like a movie reel.

JESSICA RUBEN

CHAPTER 8

VINCENT

Tom and I leave the meeting together. It's only ten at night, but I'm so tired it may as well be three in the morning.

"Let's hang out and order some food. I'm starving." He opens a pack of cigarettes, grumbling when he realizes the box is empty.

"No. I need to be alone," I tell him seriously. I keep wondering how Eve is doing. I want to run into her room and force her to talk, but I shouldn't. She has to calm down before I speak with her. And something tells me that after our discussion last night, a few days off from me is the right move.

"Vince," he says emphatically, a nervous look on his face. I cock an eyebrow. Tom only shortens my name when he's broaching a sore subject. "I still can't believe that Eve is actually here in school with us. What are the fuckin' chances? I mean, shit, I know you told me how smart she is. But there are so many other schools. I mean, fuck. Talk about a turn of events. We've gotta discuss this."

I let out a grunt. After the shit that went down between Carlos and I, I had no choice but to tell Tom about Eve and what happened between us. I needed him to do some damage control for me since I didn't kill Carlos on behalf of the family. Tom may be family, but he isn't Antonio's son, and he isn't in the inner circle—not yet, anyway. He can get away with more than I can. Ending the life of the sergeant of arms for a gang—even if it's only a pissant street gang, would be a declaration of war if it came from me.

It took a long time, but I was finally accepting Eve was good and truly gone from my life. In my head, she was off at some great school, living her dreams in safety and maybe even wearing the Uggs I bought her. And even though I felt like I gave up something bigger than the world as I knew it, I told myself that so long as she was doing well, it was enough for me. It had to be. I'd eventually get out from under Daniela's thumb, get off the East Coast, and maybe one day, have a chance with Eve again.

But all that came crashing down around me when I saw her at the party last night. I seriously just couldn't believe it. And God, she's so beautiful. I wish I kept her in my bed, head on my pillow, body wrapped up in my sheets. She should be with me, not in some cold dorm room. Instead, I sent her off like the asshole that I am after mauling the hell out of her. She must be mortified, thinking that I used her. With the life she grew up with, what else would she believe?

Tom clears his throat. "Let's stop at that deli. I need a fresh pack of smokes." He throws the empty pack in the trashcan on the corner as we step into the dimly lit bodega. The place is tiny and jam-packed with rows of junk food. There's a small counter in the corner selling lotto tickets and cigarettes.

"Can I help you?" The clerk looks between us nervously, probably grabbing his gun beneath the register. The truth is, he should be afraid. We're both huge—sucking the air out of this place and making it look more like a dollhouse than a store. We're also packing some serious heat tonight. I've got four guns and a knife on my body, all concealed. Although we do our best to tone it down when we're out in the real world, we're always Borignone mafia. We could set this entire place on fire and get away with it. We're dominant in this city, and everyone knows it.

Tom leans against the counter, giving his best smile to put the clerk at ease. "Marlboro Lights." Tom reaches into his back pocket and pulls out his leather wallet that we bought together in Buenos Aires last year. Dropping a hundred-dollar bill on the counter, the guy hands him his pack and opens the register to get him his change.

"Make that two," I interject. Tom turns to me, a smirk on his face. He pays for the packs and we head back outside.

He chuckles. "Behind that stone face you're sporting, you're really freaking the fuck out right now that she's here, huh?" Tom knows I only smoke when I'm stressed.

"Shut up, man." I open my pack while he laughs.

"Don't worry." He throws a meaty arm around my shoulder. "We'll eat and chain smoke on your balcony—and maybe we can even braid each other's hair—while we discuss the girl you killed for." He's laughing, but behind the smile, I can tell he's mad as fuck.

He moves his hands to the back of my head and I duck, shifting away from him. We walk to my building near school, talking shit until we finally get upstairs. My apartment here is a nice-sized one bedroom; it has a black leather couch, nice big screen TV, and a simple rug on the floor. It's totally different from both my room at my dad's townhouse and from my SoHo loft. In a weird way, it's appropriate though; all three sides of me are represented via different living arrangements.

Tom takes out his phone to order the pizza while I walk out onto my small balcony for a minute of privacy. I pull out another cigarette. Lighting up, I let myself take a deep inhale.

Most people in my world smoke. I try not to since I love to fight and don't want anything to slow my training down. But every so often, it feels damn good. It's completely quiet on my block, and that's by design. I can't stand the stress and hustle of the city. The truth is, I can't wait to get the hell out of here. I turn to the glass door to see Tom laying back on my couch and turning on the TV. Thank fuck. The last thing I need is for him to question me right now.

Tom and I have been Borignone family since before birth. My father grew up in Brooklyn, the American-born son of Italian immigrants. While his father didn't choose the life, two of his uncles rose to infamy in the early 1970s by taking bets on sports, eventually using their brand of muscle to manipulate games. Those uncles are the men who supported my father as he grew up. They bought him shoes when his were torn and gave him lunch money when his own father's pockets were empty. And so, after grade school, my father joined the family. And since his uncles' deaths, he's the Boss. Gambling, guns, and drugs are our main sources of income. Tom's father, Enzo, is my father's consigliere. The hope is that one day, Tom will be mine. Even though he's made, he isn't at the highest rung—yet. But I am. I've killed for the family, and I'd do a fuck of a lot worse if need be. I may be at a crossroads right now, but I'm a man of loyalty. Always will be.

What's funny is that once upon a time, being part of the family was all I ever wanted. I desired all the benefits that came with the notoriety. I knew, even then, that most men would sell their soul for a chance to live the life I was born into. They wish, if only for a moment, to walk into a cocaine den where naked women sort and weigh the goods—tits sprinkled with white powder. The vacations abroad on private planes. The non-stop cash pouring in. Hell, being above the law basically guarantees a life of debauchery. But that's just human nature, isn't it? Without being forced to tow a line, everyone would be running as wild as we are.

No other illegal enterprise is as powerful, organized, or as successful. We're the governing body of most black markets on the East Coast. Hell, Eve said it on the night we met. If the government turns a blind eye to illegal shit like fights, then control is lost and people get hurt. Well, she was wrong about something. Control isn't lost. It just falls into someone else's hands. And usually, it's ours.

I swallow hard, letting my mind wander back to the night that would change the path of my life forever.

***

We throw our blue caps in the air and cheer. Everyone slaps each other's backs, scattering to find family. My father comes to me, chuckling in both pride and amusement while one-hundred-twenty students gawk at us. People know who we are, and they stare in nervous fascination. The Mafia Don and his intellectual son; I earned my honors status. We're both well over six-feet tall with chiseled, hard features. I'm already wider and thicker than he is. Where his eyes are electric blue, mine are coal black like my Native American mother.

I graduated in the top five percent of my class, and it wasn't done with anything other than aptitude coupled with hard work. My IQ took me far, but to get to the top level here at Tri-Prep Academy, nothing but keeping my head in the books would get me the grades I needed for an Ivy League. My father always knew my potential, and he was sure to capitalize on it. If we want to take our business to the next level one day, we need someone in the family with the academic credentials. An inside man to be the face of legitimacy.

Behind all the shit we do is love and loyalty; that's what we stand for, and it's something that regular society doesn't have. These boys around me would shorten their lives to be me. I don't give a fuck how many times they shrink back, talking shit about what we do. The truth is they wish they were me.

If they had the brotherhood as I do—people who have their back no matter what—I'd bet my life they'd never leave it.

My father shakes his head, excitement in his eyes. "Tonight's the night, Vincent."

I nod, doing my best not to show how excited I truly am.

Tom moves next to me, his typically fun-loving face turning serious as he puts his hand out to my father, showing respect.

Tom never gave a shit about school and grades. He spent the last four years partying, fucking girls, and doing small-time shit for the family. Now that he's graduated, he plans to stay and work in the ports of New York and New Jersey with his father, who oversees our business there. The family dominates the waterfronts, and our stronghold could always use more loyal muscle. His father is a Capo—a made man of the highest rank, beneath my father, of course.

Most of the kids in school are getting into their limos to go to the Hamptons for post-grad parties, planning to get drunk and party. Meanwhile, my father and I step into the back of our Rolls Royce, heading to one of our warehouses in Long Island.

Sitting side by side in the back seat, my father takes a small black box from inside his suit jacket. "Open it." The warmth in my father's tone from earlier has disappeared.

I use my thumbs to pry the box open. It's a gold crucifix. I let my fingers touch the simple chain. Every member of the family wears this. Everyone's got ink, too. The Borignone insignia.

"You aren't getting inked," he says, reading my mind. I move my head in confusion. "When you're in college, you have to focus. I don't want people seeing you and automatically knowing you belong to us. You've gotta be smarter. Cleaner."

I look into his electric eyes. "Yes, sir." I keep my mouth in a firm line, my attention solely on him.

"And you don't wear this until tonight is complete."

I shut the box, sliding it into my pocket. I'm not sure what tonight will bring, but I'm ready for anything.

I may have a propensity for books, but I take my fighting and gun skills very seriously. People like to think that today's mob families are less dangerous and powerful as they once were. Well, that's an utter lie. We're just better at cloaking ourselves in legitimate work. Regardless, behind the surface of intellect and schooling, I still have my father's blood running through my veins.

During the ride, tiny pieces of doubt creep inside my head, but I shove them down, focusing on my future. It's time for me to man up and accept my destiny. Scenery passes by in a blur; before I know it, the city skyline is behind us. The traffic, as usual, is ridiculous on the Long Island Expressway. "I swear to God, Vincent." He lowers the window before taking out a cigarette and lighting up. "They could add a tenth lane to this motherfucking highway and there would still be bumper-to-bumper traffic at any hour of the day. Fucking bullshit."

"I heard the mayor is creating this traffic on purpose as punishment or some shit, for someone in the political arena for not supporting him."

My father laughs. "That's life. Tit for tat. Someone should leak that shit to the Post."

Other than that comment, he sits beside me without a sound. Completely unmoving, other than taking slow and deep drags of his cigarette. A lesser man may be afraid by his silent demeanor, by the way he's trained his eyes to show no emotion. The government would argue Antonio Borignone is an enemy of the United States. They wouldn't be wrong.

About an hour later, we step out of the car and stand in front of a huge warehouse; the combination of heat and recently smoked cigarettes permeate the air. Sweat drips down my sides, dampening my starched Armani button-down shirt.

My father opens the heavy gray door and has me walk ahead of him; I'd be lying if I said exhilaration wasn't the primary thing I feel.

The warehouse is dim and damp. We strut through towers of gun-filled wooden crates while my father's shoes clap against the concrete floors, echoing through the space.

Standing at the top of a concrete staircase, my father taps my back. I look into his eyes and he nods, telling me in his own way that what I'm about to see and do will probably change my life forever. I stare at him unblinking, communicating that I'm ready.

I move ahead of him, my steps measured as I walk down the narrow staircase.

I smell it first: a twisted mixture of piss, puke, and blood. Two young-looking guys, at least from what I can tell beneath their broken faces, sit in plastic chairs. Their arms and legs are bound together with cable ties. They're crying like little bitches, noses broken, eyes blackened and shut. Pools of liquid saturate the floor under their chairs.

"Jesus Christ," I say out loud, lip curling in disgust. A tightening sensation moves deep within my bones.

I swallow hard and take a moment to look around. All the men in the family are here, jaws tense. My heart thumps. I crack my neck from left to right, relieving the tension before moving to my knuckles.

"Finish 'em." The order leaves my father's lips as easily as if he were telling me to take out the trash.

I've beaten up plenty of guys in the past, but killing—this is something new to me. I neatly pull off my suit jacket and hand it to my father, as if I have all the time in the world. I look around the room again. If the family wants these men dead, they must have done something deserving of this ending. Borignone mafia doesn't kill for nothing. But if you fuck with one of ours, payment will be due.

I nod at the ten Capos around me, giving my respect. And then I turn to the two men seated in front of me. Before I can question myself further, I pull out my gun and steady my hands, shooting each of them directly in the head. Their brain matter splatters around them, black and red, like some fucked-up Jackson Pollock painting.

My father places his hand on my shoulder, letting me know without words, that I completed the duty. I immediately turn the safety of my gun back on, sliding it into my holster. The men's faces register pride.

"These two gangbanged Sammy's daughter out in Central Islip a few weeks ago." I open and close my fists a few times. Sammy is an associate who we all love. He isn't here tonight, of course. But I know his daughter, Allison, well. She's a thirteen-year-old girl who I would guess is on the Autism spectrum. No one talks about it since weakness isn't ever discussed within the family. Here, we only strengthen our strengths. But she and I play math games together during Sunday night dinners. I've told my father already that when she's of age, we need to get her to help us manipulate some numbers; her ability is off the damn charts. And these motherfuckers hurt her? Took advantage of a disabled child?

I pull my gun out again, shooting each of these bastards again, and again, picturing sweet Allison in my head. I wish I could revive them just to kill them again. When I'm finished, I see the back of my father's suit as he walks over to the bodies, his shiny black Ferragamos clapping against the gray concrete. He leans over the dead men, spitting on them.

"Chop 'em up before you burn the bodies," he demands. One by one, each man in the family steps up to me, shaking my hand.

Single file, we walk toward another door in the back, entering a new room. It's small and completely wood-paneled, smelling distinctly of cedar. The table in the center is huge, taking up most of the space. My father pulls out a large knife with a jewel-encrusted handle and turns to me. "This part of your induction will represent sharing of blood. This is the Family," he says, gesturing to the men around us. "Nothing else comes before it. Leaving is only possible in a coffin."

He lifts my hand, slowly slicing the center of my palm with the knife. Surprisingly, it doesn't hurt at all; my adrenaline is so high right now; I can't feel a thing. My blood beads up to the surface of my skin. Taking a piece of white parchment paper from the table, he turns my hand over, letting it drip onto the sheet. The paper is then passed from man to man until reaching my father again.

He lights a match, setting the bloodied paper aflame. "Repeat after me," he says with a nod. "Honor. Allegiance. Family." With a steady voice, I repeat the oath, sealing my fate.

"There's still a little more, Vincent." He taps my back, motioning for me to follow him again. He brings me into another room, crates piled low to the ground. The men circle me.

"We all know how fuckin' smart you are. You all know that my son graduated Tri-Prep tonight? Columbia is coming this fall." They do a slow clap at first, which turns into whistles and hollers. "Sound mind, sound body. Now, show us what you can do in the ring."

I turn my head left and right. A few men wearing ski masks walk inside the circle. I can tell by the way they move their feet that they are trained fighters. Luckily for me, I'm a machine.

The family doctor stitches me up before sending me back to the townhouse. I walk up a few floors until I get to my bathroom. Dropping to my white tile floor, I vomit into the toilet bowl.

"What have I done?" I sit up against the cold marble wall, willing my body to stop shaking. I feel my teeth chattering in my mouth, but I can't will them to stop.

Dropping my head in my hands, I roughly grab my hair. The night's events need to be compartmentalized. I'm not a pussy. I can handle this. Somehow, I force myself up to stand in front of the mirror.

I grip the sink hard, my knuckles shaking with the pressure. "I'm a made man. This is my destiny." My voice is quiet. I look at myself harder, moving closer to the glass and repeating the words. I need my brain to believe! "I'm a made man. This is my mother-fucking DESTINY!" I scream, punching the glass with my fist, shattering the mirror to pieces.

***

A taxi honks his horn and I'm brought back to the present. Shit, I need to calm the fuck down. I let an image of Eve float into my head and somehow, I exhale the tightness in my chest. It's not just how stunning she is. It's more. It's the way she moves. Thinks. Breathes. How she sees more than just the sum of my parts. When people look at me—with the family or during my fights—they see the muscles and the anger and a good-looking face. When people look at me in school, they see an image that Daniela projects. Somehow, my life has become increasingly fragmented. But with Eve? I'm whole. She's someone I can't afford to lose.

I lean against the railing when the balcony door opens It's Tom. He moves next to me, lighting up his cigarette. "Fuck, it's getting cold," he mumbles, rubbing his hands together like we're on the Titanic.

"Why don't you bring yourself a sweater from inside? Maybe make a hot chamomile tea while you're at it?"

He laughs. "Erez is coming in from Israel next week. How many men of his do you think we'll need? They'll have to be ready by spring."

"I expect things to be pretty tense when we get there. I already know the Tribal Council isn't down with us partnering up with them. We may need around fifty guys to convince them otherwise."

Tom exhales smoke. "Fuck, yeah. It's time to take what's ours." He spits off the balcony. "Don't let that bitch derail us now, true? You've gotta keep your head on the prize. You've got to be all about *your* girl right now. And I don't mean the tiny one with the big brown eyes. I mean the snake with red hair and claws."

"Yeah." I flick some ash off the balcony. The lie burning my throat. There's no way in hell I'm going to have Eve near me and not make her mine.

"So, you won't talk to her anymore?" He drops his cigarette on the concrete balcony floor, stepping on it with his shoe. "I know your vague answers. You say 'yeah yeah yeah,' but in the end, you always do whatever the fuck you wanna do." His voice is harder now.

"Think before you speak, brother," I reply firmly, daring him with my eyes to spew more bullshit at me. We stare at each other wordlessly, aggression fueling our stances.

"Fuck, Vince!" he seethes, stepping closer to me. "Swear to me you'll stay away from her! We've got plans. The family needs you to stay on the path. Shit between you and Eve almost ruined everything for us last year. Since that bitch, you can't even be with another girl! You know I've been telling you that it feels like a storm is brewing at the ports. On top of that, we can't be left with this much dirty cash. It's a bad recipe."

I grab his shirt, lifting him to my face. "Don't call her a bitch."

"Calm the fuck down," he yells. "I'm not the enemy!"

I try to blink the rage out of my vision. When I finally let go, he shakes out his shoulders, still fuming.

"She's turned you inside out. You don't want any pussy other than hers? Fine. Keep being a damn monk. You used to fuck a different girl every night!"

"Who I fuck is none of your goddamn business!"

"That's where you're wrong." He steps up. "That fake relationship you've got going on with Daniela directly affects all of us. We aren't done with her yet. And we both know that if you cut shit off with her too soon, we'll be up in a shit storm. You know how long they could put us away for?" His voice tempers at the end, but it does nothing to chill my anger.

My lips curl in fury. "Don't fuckin' lecture me. You think I don't know every detail of what you're talking about? I've got it under control. Whatever is going on with Eve has nothing to do with *this*!" I breathe heavily.

His eyes widen and he lets out a cackle. "Control? You find a girl with a face wars are fought over, and you think you can pull off *control*?"

"Yes. For her, I will do whatever it takes. Once I get this shit off the ground in Nevada—"

"You know what? You aren't thinking." He starts breathing hard, gripping the railing in rage. "Eve will cause a clusterfuck for the family. Let. Her. Go. You think you can keep a relationship alive with Daniela while having Eve? It's hard enough for you to be fake with Daniela right now, despite the fact that you haven't fucked her in ages. Your temper with her is borderline abusive. Three weeks ago at that charity event? The photos of the two of you don't look fucking convincing. Daniela will catch wind of another woman, brother. And when she does, there will be hell to pay for all of us."

"I'll talk to Eve. I'll explain everything, and she'll get it."

"That girl's got her finger hooked into your heart, and getting reacquainted with her again after working so hard on trying to move on, is going to fuck. You. Up." He looks at me with an incensed expression and I turn to him with an even angrier one.

"Don't talk to me like that, motherfucker. Not now, and not ever!" I take a heavy step toward him, and Tom immediately shuffles back. Instead of hitting him like I ache to do, I pull out another cigarette and light up.

"You don't give a fuck about anything but that girl. That much is clear."

I stare at his ashen face, taking another step closer until we're barely an inch apart. I use my height to my advantage, staring down at him.

"The family always comes first, but I'll never be fucking done with her. Understand? Never. I will walk through fire to keep her. And the next time you question me and my authority, I'll break your fucking face." My voice is quiet, but the rage simmers beneath my skin.

"Well, you'll have to walk through shit worse than fire in prison, 'cause that's where you'll be if you can't keep your dick in your pants and eye on the prize. Until we get our new business running, there are no other options."

The doorbell rings. Tom turns from me, stepping back into the apartment and sliding the balcony door shut behind him. I watch as he opens the front door and hands the delivery guy some cash from his back pocket. Dropping the pie on the coffee table, he opens the door and pops his head into the balcony again. "Hey fucker, come in and let's eat."

I walk back inside and we dig in, our conversation shelved for now. I'm biting into a hot slice, my mind running rampant when his phone pings. He lifts it off the coffee table to read the text. "Wanna fight tonight?" He looks me up and down, my posture rigid. "Looks like you could let out some steam." He raises his brows and leans back on the couch, crossing his feet on the coffee table and biting into his pizza.

I nod my head. "Fuck yeah."

Three hours later, I'm in the basement of some underground warehouse, kicking the shit out of some faceless guy. And man, does it feel good.

JESSICA RUBEN

CHAPTER 9

EVE

My entire day passes in a blur. I clean my dorm room and then get to studying. Before I know it, it's nearing five o'clock. I need to wash up and get dressed before Janelle comes. After showering and putting myself together as decently as I can, I hear a knock at my door. I swing it open and see my beautiful sister, blonder than usual.

"Nice hair!" My head pounds with nerves, but I want to keep it together until it's time to fess up.

"Thanks. I felt like lightening it up a few days ago." She fluffs her roots with her fingertips as she struts into the room, her black booties clapping on the wooden floors. "I can't wait to rearrange all the furniture."

Janelle is so creative; I'm sure she'll find a way to maximize my space. Our tiny room in the Blue Houses could have been horrible. But between her little touches and the way she set up our beds and my desk, she was able to transform the space into a small oasis. "Well, what do you think we should do with the place?"

"First of all, we need to push the beds together and make you a king. Then, we can ask your RA to get rid of this extra desk." She walks to the door, staring at the room from a different angle. "Should we do Target or Bed Bath for fresh bedding? Honestly, Eve, I'm sick of looking at those old sheets. They're old and full of shitty memories."

My eyes widen. "Janelle, I don't want to spend—"

She puts her hand up. "Je-sus, Eve. Stop with that shit! It's not that expensive, and knowing you, you probably haven't spent a dime of your grant money for anything other than books. That money is meant for you to actually live! I've been doing well in tips, too. You're buying yourself new sheets and maybe even a few pillows for the big bed we're about to set up for you. And then we'll reorganize the room and order in some takeout! Oh—maybe we should get you a small table too, with two chairs? There's room for that now."

"Here we go…" I say under my breath, nervous that Janelle is going to take this whole room rearrangement to an absurdly expensive degree.

"Now sit down. Let me put you together before we leave." I drop into the seat at my desk, knowing that with Janelle, there is no room for negotiation. Luckily, it only takes her a few minutes to apply eyeliner, mascara, and a little blush on my face. Moments later, we're knocking on my resident advisor's door to make a small request before heading to Bed Bath and Beyond.

"Oh, hey Eve." Her usual animated self is on display; I squint my eyes at her yellow polo shirt with the collar popped, and her matching hair ribbon. Alexandra is a brand of New England preppy that I never knew existed until college. My sister turns to me, furrowing her brow as if to say, *is this bitch for real?*

"Hey, Alexandra," I reply in my perkiest voice. "Now that I don't have a roommate, I was hoping you could have someone remove that second desk?" Janelle turns to me, her eyes widening at my tone, but I ignore her.

"Of course." She nods happily, ponytail swaying. "I'll call housing services tonight."

Janelle squeezes my hand three times and then turns to Alexandra. "Thanks for your help, sweetie." Her tone is so upbeat and unnatural that I have to bite my cheek not to laugh.

"No problem!" she exclaims, thankfully not understanding that Janelle is mocking her. She gently shuts the door and we turn down the hallway.

We're barely ten feet away when Janelle starts cracking up. "Seriously? Whatever Kool-Aid that bitch drinks, I need a sip a' that!" We continue our snickering as we walk out of the building.

Forty minutes later, we're arguing over king-sized sheet colors and plastic table sizes. Luckily, we manage to leave the store without tearing each other apart. Janelle is holding overflowing bags of jersey sheets in navy—while clutching pillows, a duvet puffy-thing to go inside a navy-and-white floral cover—along with a cute little area rug in silver that she tells me I absolutely need. Meanwhile, I'm hauling a small white plastic table, folded, and two white plastic folding chairs.

We get in a large taxi that fits all of our goods in its trunk and head back to my dorm. We both break into a sweat as we drop all of the new stuff by the door. They had delivery, but neither of us wanted to waste the twenty bucks.

After taking a breath and drinking some water from the sink, we get to the heavy work of pushing the single beds together in order to turn it into a king, pushing both to the left side of the room. Janelle answers the knock at the door and it's two big guys from student services here to remove the spare desk.

"Oh, hey guys," Janelle says with a sugary smile as she lowers her eyes, getting a nice long look at their denim-clad asses. I roll my eyes at her blatant ogling and can't help myself but laugh; I do a cursory glance and have to say, they look pretty good in those jeans. Not like Vincent, but—I quickly turn my head and breathe through the pain. Thoughts of him now are accompanied by agony.

She hops up onto the desk that's staying and crosses one long leg over the other. "So, are you guys students here?" She cocks her head to the side, her eyes twinkling with mischief. The guy with blue eyes stares back at her, clearly liking what he sees.

"Yeah," he shrugs. "We just do this shit for a little extra cash on the side." His accent is all Brooklyn.

Janelle turns to me, eyes wide. "You see, Eve? Everyone here isn't a spoiled rich kid!" I want to glare at her, but the guys laugh, and so I do too. After chatting for a few minutes about the uptight and spoiled kids at school, Janelle takes their phone numbers and they leave the room with the spare desk.

We clean up the dust from the corners of the room and Janelle finally unrolls the new area rug. My old sheets and comforter are now in a huge trash bag. Looking around my room, I'm in a state of utter surprise. "This looks amazing, Janelle!"

"Hell yeah, it does." She holds out her fist for me to pound and we knock them together saying "swish" at the end. It's a stupid handshake, but we both love it, so we do it anyway.

I clear my throat, knowing we're going to have to talk. I've got a shitload of stuff to unload on her tonight, and it won't be pretty.

"I'll order the Chinese. And then... we talk."

She's texting someone on her phone while she replies to me. "Make sure to get some spicy sesame noodles. The girls I live with barely eat a thing. Do you see how skinny I've gotten?" She tries to look appalled as she stares at her bony arm, but I know that she's actually thrilled.

"I can see your bones," I reply in all seriousness.

"Really?" She jumps up and down with glee.

"You're crazy; you know that?" I can't help but chuckle at her exuberance.

"Well, everyone can't just eat their faces off and be all perfect like you, you bitch." She winks. "Now, order that food before I eat you."

I roll my eyes as I place the order. I decided I'd better wait until she's full before I give her the Vincent saga.

The delivery guy comes and goes, and we sit at the small table to dig in.

"You see? I told you this was necessary!" She spears a piece of chicken with her fork and takes a bite.

"I've got shit to tell you, Janelle." I look down at the food I've yet to touch and finally lift my face to hers. My eyes must show anguish because she stops chewing.

"All right. Lay it on me," she says as she swallows her last bite. "Some bitches giving you trouble? Because if they are, I have no problem kicking someone's ass."

I swallow hard, gathering the nerve. "No. But, Janelle, I'm going to tell you something kind of serious. And you have to swear not to be angry that I've…withheld all of it from you. But before I start, I want you to know that it's all over now. So really, there isn't a reason I'm telling you this except that I feel like you ought to know."

"Oh, shit. You're babbling. That's a bad sign. What is it?" Her no-nonsense stare propels me forward. Before I know it, I'm telling her every gritty detail I've kept close to my heart about Vincent. Once I start, I can't seem to stop myself. I thought that saying it all out loud would push everything farther from me. But it turns out, the opposite occurs. Talking about him and what we had only makes the entirety of my memories more vivid.

The dinner and club the night we met. Making out in the stairwell. Ice skating. I include the information about Angelo's pawnshop when I met Antonio. Hell, I say it all. I don't think I've ever talked so much in my life. When I'm done, Janelle sits completely frozen, staring at me with an expressionless face. For what it's worth, it felt amazing to unload. But watching the way her face is morphing into hurt and fury, I know I'm about to pay.

She blinks her eyes a few times. "So, you're telling me, that *the Bull* is actually Vincent Borignone? And he killed Carlos. For you. And now he's at Columbia. Here. But it turns out that he's had a girlfriend all along—and she's some billionaire's daughter and she's gorgeous and connected and all over social media? And last night you guys made out, but he stopped you. And he told you he loves you and that he wants to explain everything..."

I shuffle in my seat, gathering myself. "Um, I guess that's the general r-rundown..." I stutter.

"So, you're telling me," she repeats a little louder. "That you never touched a man in your life other than making out with Juan. And then you almost had sex with Vincent Borignone. And you never told me?"

"Well, I was never technically *with* him..." My voice sounds tiny to my own ears. "But, I didn't know who he was at the time..."

"Eve. Look into my eyes right now!" she exclaims. "Whatever is between you and him is O.V.E.R." She punctuates every letter, making sure I understand. "Am I being clear? That motherfucking killer isn't allowed anywhere near you."

"Janelle, I think you're—"

"Don't say I'm overreacting," she says angrily.

I turn my head to the door and then back to her. "Shhh! Someone might hear you!"

She takes a breath to calm herself down, but the anger is still slick on her tongue. "No fuckin' way. No, Eve. You don't realize what's happening. You're too naïve." She throws her arms up in the air. "This man is fucking dangerous." She stands up, pacing back and forth in the room. "I don't give a rat's ass if he's so smart that he wins that stupid No-Bell Prize or whatever the fuck it's called. He is bad news. He should not be ANY news. Vincent Borignone is Antonio's son." Her words come out staccato, she's panting, talking a mile a minute. "I never knew he was the Bull, but I've heard his name a million times. He's dangerous as all fuck. He'll probably be running the family one day."

She keeps moving, on a rampage. "He isn't an associate like our Angelo. He's a *made man*. You thought the Snakes were bad? The Cartel?" Her breathing turns rapid. "Holy fuck Eve, this man is a hundred times those guys." She sits back down, grabbing my hands in hers. "Swear to me right now that you will never. Ever. Speak to him again."

"Janelle..." My heart is pounding. I know that everything she is saying is the truth. But it hurts.

"Last week Vania, whose boyfriend works in the fish market by the docks, told her that everyone pays the Borignones. Anything moved through the waterfront is taxed by them. And what do you think happens if someone says *no*?"

I sit in silence as she continues.

"No talking. No looking. Whatever that shit was you had between the two of you is over. And, do you realize what he turned you into last year? How you could even think of defending him right now—is making my stomach turn."

Visions of my mother being a mistress to these rich guys flash through my mind. How many times was my mother the one they all made promises to? They swore they were ending their marriages. They promised her a new apartment. They swore everything under the sun. But inevitably, it all would blow up in her face.

"You want to be the side piece to Vincent Borignone?" she continues. "Because that's what he wants. It's what all powerful men like him want. He's got that fancy piece of ass he takes around town. She's the public one. She's the one with the life and the kids and the Mercedes Benz. You're the idiot on the side! It's all fun and games until he's got you on a fucking leash, living in his high-rise penthouse on Park Avenue until the day he gets sick of you. He'll handcuff you emotionally to him, and meanwhile, you'll never get to live your own life!"

I gasp as if I've been slapped. Janelle is hitting on every insecurity I've ever had. "It's n-not like that," I say, my voice breaking. A headache sets in the back of my skull; a pounding pain that's growing by the second.

She opens her eyes wider. "Yeah. It's exactly like that. He saw you as some charity case. Okay, maybe he's attracted to you. But he will never choose you over her, Eve. Ne-ver." She snaps, crosses her arms over her chest.

"You can't understand what we had—he swore there's more than it seems! And—Carlos—"

"Stop making excuses." Her eyes move wildly. "Let me be clear. Number one." She lifts a perfectly manicured finger in the air. "He's got a girlfriend. He had a girlfriend while he was hooking up with you and he cheated with you—on her. And I don't care that he didn't fuck you when he obviously could have. I mean shit, Eve! Did you listen to yourself recount the story?"

She lifts a second finger in the air. "And secondly, he's Vincent fucking Borignone. He's a killer. He fucking kills people for the mafia. Are you listen-ing to me? How do you even know that he killed Carlos for you? Maybe it was because the Snakes were rising in power and he had to take care of him?"

My stomach sinks. I know I have to hear it, and here it is.

"I'm serious, Eve. I refuse to allow this. I'm putting my foot down. If you can't stay away from him—or if he doesn't stay away from you—I'm calling Angelo. And I know for a fact he will go fucking insane on your ass. We all didn't bend backward for the past four years only to have you back in bed with the enemy!"

My face feels like it's burning as tears stream down my cheeks.

She lets out a sigh, her voice softening. "You can't let him do this to you." She gently pushes some hair off my face. "You can do better than him, Eve. I know it. A man like him will seriously fuck you up. The money and the power is an easy thing to get lost in. But at the end of the day, a man like him sees a girl like you or me, they see where we came from, and they try to take advantage. They make false promises. They lie—"

"He has a girlfriend. I know that. I stalked the hell out of them. I lived my life running from these gangs. The streets. I'm done with that and I'm done with him. It's over. Done," I say as she looks at me pointedly as if she isn't sure she believes me. "It's over and done, Janelle. I promise."

"Well, halle-fuckin'-lujah. It's not like you saw him all that much anyway, right?"

I drop my head. Our timeline may have been short in the way we normally think about time, as twenty-four hours a day. But the way time managed to move with us was…different. Heavier. Deeper. *More*.

CHAPTER 10

EVE

It's Monday morning. I walk into my economics class, taking a seat in the center of the lecture hall. Jared, a starter for the school's football team, drops into the chair next to mine, giving me a grin that has most of the girls in class swooning. The girls on my floor put him on our hottest guys list and seeing him so close like this, it's obvious why. With his shaggy blond hair and sparkling blue eyes, he looks like the perfect farm boy who could probably tip a cow over with one of his bulging muscles.

After talking to Janelle last night, I realize I need to force myself to move on. I know Vincent said he wants us to discuss it, but there's no way in hell I'm doing that. God knows, my pain threshold has been reached.

"So, Eve, how's the year going for you?"

"It's cool," I say with a smile, opening up my red spiral notebook and pulling out a pen from my backpack. Almost everyone in class is sitting with a laptop open in front of them, but I find that it's harder to concentrate with a computer screen in front of me. Instead, I take handwritten notes in class and then type them on my laptop once I'm back in my room. It's probably overkill, but it's been working for me so far.

"Do you live in the quad?" His smile reaches his eyes. Jared's got swag, I'll give him that. He's really good-looking in that all-American way. I know I should feel excited, but I don't feel any zing. I take a deep breath, pushing these stupid thoughts away. What is a "zing" anyway? Zings are for naïve girls who don't know better.

I shrug my shoulders, feeling inexplicably shy. "Yeah, I do. Are you there, too?" I give him my best smile.

"Yeah." He's looking at me with blatant interest and I want to kick myself right now for not enjoying the moment. Guilt sits like a pit in the back of my throat. Why am I feeling this? I need someone to give me the Heimlich.

He shifts his thick, muscular arm so that it's flush against mine, and an irrational prickle of anxiety moves through me. I should feel thrilled, not frightened. Vincent must have changed my DNA or something. Now that my body knows a man like him exists, nothing else is a match. Everything else feels blatantly wrong. He set himself up as a benchmark for what a man should be; he was so damn impactful, he managed to change my vision for any other man. How am I going to get past that? Past him?

Luckily, the professor begins his lecture and I force myself to concentrate. Jared and I make eyes a few times while the professor talks and the truth is that it feels good to be wanted. And even if I still think about Vincent, I know my actions will *never* follow through with what's happening in my head. I won't allow it; I'm stronger than that. So, a new guy who is single and normal? Bring it on! I can add him to my list titled: Fake it 'til I make it.

Class is finally over. I slide my books into my backpack, laughing about something funny Jared says when I feel my skin prickle. I move my head up and immediately spot him. Vincent's striding toward me, confidently, as if he was expecting to see me here. A piece of his hair falls into his eye, but nothing can cover that piercing gaze. He's a hunter, and I'm the deer about to get speared.

Jared is completely oblivious to Vincent's approach as he gathers his books. I want to grab him and beg him to take me with him out of the classroom before Vincent reaches me. My heart thuds as Vincent steps right between us, ignoring Jared's existence as if he was nothing more than dust.

"Uh, bye Eve." Jared waves as he scurries away. Vincent leans against my desk, his eyes practically black.

"Who the fuck was that?" he asks angrily.

"You're joking, right?" I lift my backpack up on the table and open the zipper roughly. I drop my books inside, shutting it as if the zipper and I are mortal enemies.

"I know you're angry." His voice is gruff. I don't reply to him, because I can't. My voice literally won't work right now. I'm too hurt.

Vincent looks around the now-empty lecture hall. Grabbing my hand, he pulls me out of the room and into the hallway.

"What the hell, Vincent. Stop!" I whisper yell.

Of course, he doesn't even pause. He practically drags me behind his enormous body. With every step we take, my anger amplifies. He's handling me like I'm nothing more than a doll, and I'm tired of it. I'm a human being, not a tool to use whenever he feels like it. We finally stop in a quiet corridor.

"Fuck you!" I shout. The emotional pain ripping through my chest is so acute, I can feel my entire face turning red.

He tries to take my hand, but I ball it into a fist so he can't hold it. "Look," he huffs. "How about we go get a late lunch and talk about it. Let's figure it all out, okay? Are you hungry?" His voice is measured as if he expected this outburst from me. But I can't manage to calm myself down. The anger is too fresh. All of a sudden, another burst of indignation moves through my body. *I'm not taking his shit anymore.*

"I'm not a cheater. And I'm not a lunatic either to be dating the son of Antonio Borignone. I came here because it's one of the best schools in the country and I'm not ruining my life because of you. There is nothing we need to discuss." I take a heaving breath. "The. End."

He bends down to get closer to me and lowers his voice. "You're coming out with me, and we're talking."

"No, we are not." I turn my head, making sure no one is near us. The last thing I need is to be part of the Vincent gossip mill. "Actually, I have an idea. Go to lunch with your girlfriend of the past few years and be sure to snap a photo with your shirt off while you're at it. I'm sure your leeeeegions of fans would looooove to see The Vincent Borignone shirtless. And when you're done with her, go see your father and maybe shoot someone for not giving you a cut of their profits!"

He stares at me wide-eyed before bursting out laughing, which only makes me more furious. "Come on, Eve. How can I not laugh? You're funny."

"Funny?" If I were in a cartoon, smoke would be billowing out of my ears right now. I turn my body around, ready to walk away.

"Hey," he says, stepping forward so I'm pressed against the wall. "There's a lot about the situation you don't know. And yeah, she likes to post shit about us, but it never mattered much to me before. Let's go out. Let me just explain—"

"Before? Before what? Before or after you put me in your goddamn bed?" I shouldn't be speaking to him right now. I watch as resolve comes over his face. I'm about to yell again when he bends down and picks me up, throwing me over his enormous shoulder.

I want to scream, but I don't want to draw attention to us as we walk out of the corridor. My hair is dangling down, practically sweeping the floor. And for the first time in my life, I'm relieved that it's so thick and riotous because it's covering my face from any potential passerby. He's carrying me like a caveman and I'm absolutely powerless. If people are staring, I wouldn't know; my eyes are screwed shut. When I realize he isn't going to put me down without a fight, I try to pinch his side. Not only is he not ticklish, but he's a solid wall of muscle without an ounce of fat to grab. My voice is low as I threaten his life, but he completely ignores me. Blood rushes to my head and I stay quiet, hoping he'll flip me back over soon.

We get to the student parking lot, filled with fancy looking cars. Lowering his body and placing my feet on the ground, he holds my arms to make sure I don't fall over. When I'm stable, he puts his hands through my crazy hair, acting like he's doing me a favor by taming it.

"Your hair is wild, Eve." He's cackling, and I want to strangle him with my bare hands.

"Thanks a lot, jackass. Everyone can't have perfectly silky hair like you. I can't imagine how much you probably pay for conditioner. You probably get it cut at the salon Janelle's at, paying two-hundred-and-fifty bucks for a trim."

He guffaws, shaking his head in amazement. "I love this side of you," he smiles, checking me out from my toes up to my face. "Actually, from a certain angle with your face all flushed and your hair all crazy, it kind of looks like you've just been –"

"SHUT UP!" I yell, grabbing a clip from the bottom of my shirt. Before I can put it up, he stops me, his face turning serious. All of a sudden, things get quiet.

"Leave it. I want to see you just like this."

My breath catches as he strokes my cheek with his calloused thumb.

Letting me go, he casually walks to the driver's side of his gorgeous black Range Rover, my bag still draped over his shoulder. He gets in the car, immediately lowering the passenger-side window.

"Get in," his voice commands. I lick my lips and take a breath. I have two choices. I can either run and leave my backpack, or get in the car. Clearly, he won't take *no* for an answer. I think I have to run. I watch him unbuckle his seat belt and I freeze in my tracks. He steps out, walking back around the car.

"You think you can run away from me?" He's got a glint in his eye that's so sexy and arrogant; I'd slap the ego off his face if I could. I look behind us, trying to map out a route.

"Don't map out a route," he says, reading my mind perfectly with his ridiculously deep eyes.

"Stop reading my mind, Vincent! What the hell?" I stomp my foot on the ground like a petulant child. And because I want to do the opposite of what he thinks, I get into the front seat. I try to shut the door, but fail to pull hard enough. Again, I open and shut it with a loud slam. Finally, I put my hair up just to spite him. There!

Maybe it's good I'm going. I can finally tell him that this is the last time he's seeing me. Closure, right? Maybe once we talk, he'll leave me alone, and I can just get on with my life. Damn his perfect body and amazing face and brilliant mind.

We zip around campus until he pulls up to one of the older gothic-style libraries. We walk inside; the place is dim, covered in yellow light. The ceilings are so high and daunting. Even though it's completely silent, I can hear the walls talk: brilliant minds have studied at these desks. I want to touch all of the books, flip through their soft, yellowed pages—and imagine who must have studied here before me. I feel…lucky.

He walks us into the elevator and we exit on the fifth floor. We walk past the stacks and enter a study room.

I move to the corner of the room and watch dumbly as he shuts the door behind him. His phone rings, momentarily startling me. He immediately pulls it out from his jacket.

"Yes," he states seriously, clenching his fists. I watch as his normally dark gaze morphs to threatening. This Vincent is straight-up deadly. "I'm going to have to deal with this later. I've got an important meeting right now." He hangs up the phone and rolls out his shoulders, obviously trying to let go of whatever that call was about. Finally, he sits down. Staring at me, he's waiting for me to take a seat. I sit, keeping my back straight.

I need to start before he does. "Vincent, you've got a girlfriend, who I've been told will make my life a living hell if she sees us together. A girlfriend who has apparently been on your arm for years. And"—my temper rises—"how could you lie all that time about who you are and what you've been doing! I trusted you…I—"

"Eve," he states succinctly. "There's a lot I'm going to tell you. But if you want to rail at me first, be my guest." He leans back into his chair, crossing a huge leg over his opposite knee.

My jaw drops. Screw that! I'm not letting him set the rules. He doesn't get to tell me when I can be angry.

"You know what? No. I'm not yelling at you." I move my arms over my chest.

He reaches out, placing a hand in the center of the table. "You ready to hear it?"

"Why should I trust you? You swore you'd never lie to me." I'm surprised to see the torment on his face.

"I withheld. I told you as much as I could. Do you remember the stress you were under? How could I pile more shit on your plate?"

I shut my eyes, unable to look at him. That night I found a dead cat on my doorstep was terrifying. And Vincent saved me. But then, why? How? How could—

"Eve. Stop letting your mind go crazy. You know me. What we have is something entirely different. You know this," he begs.

"The world thinks you're the golden couple! What does that make me, Vincent?" He flinches at the desperation in my voice.

"No. Don't say that. You were never the girl on the side." He reaches out to me again, but I pull my hand away. "Eve—"

"Don't!" I turn my face away. "I'm here to tell you that we won't be seeing each other anymore. The whole thing is too fucked-up. I know who you are. And we both know what I had to do to get myself out of that hell I was living in. I'm not getting sucked back in! You made me believe you cared about me, and…" I take in a breath and swallow. "I was so afraid at that time when really, you were the one I should have been afraid of."

I look down at the floor, gathering myself.

He moves forward in his chair. "Eve, don't play that game with me. You may be innocent in a lot of ways, but you weren't exactly stopping me when I told you I'd take care of Carlos. You must have known that I had some reach."

"Don't you throw that in my face! I had no choice, and—" I let out a dark laugh. "I thought you were the better option than the Borignone family that Angelo was begging me to reach, how should I have known that you *were* the family?" My chest aches as the words leave my mouth.

"Yeah. And big bad Vincent took care of Carlos for you, didn't he?" He pushes himself back from the chair, looking up at the ceiling for a moment. "Let me go back to the beginning. You know now that I'm Borignone mafia.

My father is Antonio, and I'm his only son. We do a lot of illegal shit and make a ton of cash doing it. A few years ago…" he continues, explaining the details of Daniela's father, Alexander Costa, and how his bank houses and launders the family money.

When he finally gets into the topic of Daniela, I can't help but drop my head. "Don't tune out, Eve. We were never exclusive. At the time, she was the one I was screwing around with in school. But right after I met you, I felt like I couldn't keep living the lie. Business is one thing. But I wanted real. I wanted more. I wanted—you." He throws his hands up in the air. "The faceless and the nameless girls. Daniela's constant manipulations. I put a stop to it."

I slide my hand to the center of the table; he recognizes the offering and gently places his hand on top of mine while he continues to tell the rest to me. All the grimy details of why he's stuck pretending to be her boyfriend in public make me feel ill. My heart actually aches for him, being forced to be near such a vile human. But he clearly has no other option right now.

"So, you're saying you haven't touched her in all this time?"

He nods his head sincerely, and I swallow hard, my mouth drying. I need a moment to process all of this new information. I meet his eyes and something passes between us; it's a magnetic energy that is impossible to stop.

"There's more. You know that I'm half Native American." I furrow my brows, confused why he's reminding me of this.

I hum my assent.

"There are tribal lands in Nevada that rightfully belong to me because of my birthright. Well, technically, they are lands that belong to the entire Masuki Tribe. But I'm part of them."

There are so many questions I need to ask, and I have to trust my inner voice more. I must learn to speak up. But before I can get a word out, he continues.

"I've got a plan to develop a hotel and casino complex. Seven men run the Masuki Tribal Council right now. I mean, shit, the place is a wasteland with nothing other than a few rundown gas stations and some trailers. I want to get out there and build out a resort to rival the current Vegas strip. All the bells and whistles and amenities, but minus the tacky glitz. Totally legitimate. And on the side, I will launder family money, too. And get us away from Costa's hold."

"Does your father know?" I ask, wide-eyed.

"Of course. I started thinking about it last year after I met you, and I've been doing the legwork ever since. It will be huge in scale, and I will be the one building and then running it. Most of the planning has been done on paper. I'm just waiting to graduate before I make the move and put the plan in motion."

I fixate on the smell of old books, trying to keep my emotions calm when a memory pops into my head. "The day I saw you around the corner when I was leaving work. And you took me out for pizza. You were at the meeting at Angelo's pawn, right?"

He nods his head in the affirmative. "I'm not ordinary, Eve. As Antonio's son, I'm not just a simple soldier who can come and go as I please. This has been my path since I was born." His eyes seem to swim with misery as he states this fact.

"And th-this is what you want?" My heart beats on overtime. I want him to say *no*. I want him to say he plans to leave the life behind—because I can't have him if he's Borignone mafia. I've worked too hard in my life to come back to this, no matter how much I love him. It helps that I've lived how I've lived. Violence and drugs aren't new to me. I just never thought I'd be here. This is exactly what I've been running from. I wanted to get away from this life, yet somehow, it has followed me. How can I turn back now?

He stands up from the chair and paces the room, stopping at the glass partition and leaning his hands on the sill, facing away from me. All I can see is the large expanse of his back, and I yearn to step behind him, put my hands around his waist, and press my nose into his shirt. Instead, I grip the arms of my chair.

He turns to me, his face settled in a grim line. "The choice has already been made for me, Eve. I'm made. This is my path. But understand that when I leave the East Coast, the heat will lessen. We aren't like these shitty street gangs. Being cloaked in legitimacy is necessary. And I'll be the face of that honest business."

My head lightens as he squeezes my hand on the table, leaning forward and looking at me pleadingly. "I'll be building something real, Eve. Taxpaying citizen. Yes, I have a gun. I'm armed. That's how it is for me. And, as of now, I have no choice but to continue being her "—he pauses for a breath—"fake boyfriend. Acting like we're together, in public. But Eve," he continues. "Our relationship is completely contrived. Do you hear me? She knows it, and I know it. She just insists on looking like a couple for her image. But once I leave, we can be free."

"Can't you just find her someone else? Maybe if she had another boyfriend, she'd leave you alone." I feel desperate and angry.

He huffs at my comment, seemingly annoyed. "You think I haven't tried that?" I've attempted everything, but apparently, she thinks that having me is important for her image."

I feel my anger rise up; the injustice of it all forces the words out of my mouth. "But if you act like her boyfriend…tell her you're her boyfriend…and everyone on earth believes you're her boyfriend… Then, I'm confused why you think you aren't? You are what you do and nothing else, Vincent. If I went to school to be a lawyer, practice law, hand out business cards that say 'Eve Petrov, Esquire,' can I now say I'm not really a lawyer?"

"I will start the new business and then I will cut her loose. That's it. And your metaphor isn't appropriate, because *boyfriend* and *girlfriend* implies sexual relations, which we don't have. It also implies fidelity, which we don't have either. As far as she and I are concerned, the relationship between us is in name only. She doesn't care who I fuck, so long as the girl doesn't infringe on the public image. That's all there is."

I drop my head. "What are you doing to me, Vincent? I'm not like these girls you know. I don't have brass emotions. I can't hear one thing, see another, and stay strong through it. And I can't navigate this complicated social stuff... I'm not made that way."

"Don't you know, from the minute I met you, it has only been you?" He moves his hands to gently cover mine, and I find it difficult to breathe. "I can't even smell anyone but you…touch a woman who isn't you…" He lifts his hand and caresses the side of my face while I shut my eyes tightly. "And no one, no one has ever turned me on like you…"

The door of the study room opens. I feel a gust of cold air as Vincent's hand moves off mine at lightning speed.

We turn our heads at the same moment and I look up, staring into the ice-cold face of Daniela—shining dark red hair down past her perky boobs, tight white V-neck shirt, cropped navy leather jacket, tight skinny jeans and heels—and a look on her face that says she wants to tear me apart.

"Hello." Her smile is tight as her eyes dart between Vincent and me, finally stopping on my face. Licking her pink lips, she presses them together angrily. "I had no idea you knew my boyfriend. Wait, what was your name again? Evelyn?" She tilts her head to the side, putting a hand on Vincent's back, possessively.

I blink a few times, not sure what to say. I introduced myself at the party, but I'm obviously forgettable.

Vincent sits up in his chair. "Daniela, this is Eve. She's a freshman. Eve, this is my girlfriend, Daniela." Vincent looks at me coldly. Just a moment ago he was an open telephone line, and Daniela just put a finger on the disconnect button.

She sidles closer to him; in front of me is the best-looking couple I've ever seen. They're perfect together. I cower in my seat, feeling awkward in my Target clothing—the one who doesn't belong.

Daniela turns to him, hand massaging his neck. "Vincent, what are you doing here, anyway? Don't you usually go to the gym Monday afternoons?" Her voice is accusing.

He leans into his chair confidently, turning his face away from mine completely. "Yeah, well, Eve has been hanging out with Tom. She's having a tough time in Ancient Philosophy, and he asked me to help her out."

"Wait, your Tom?" she says disbelievingly, moving her hair over her slender right shoulder.

"Yeah. Tom. They met at Cohen's party Saturday."

My heart starts to pound. *Tom? What?* "Eve and I decided to get to know each other some before we cracked our books open. You remember how hard Ancient Philosophy is, don't you? And the start of the semester is the worst." He leans back and puts his hands behind his head casually as if he's got nothing to hide. Meanwhile, she continues to stare at the two of us skeptically.

"Hey," Vincent says to Daniela with a honeyed smile, bringing her attention back to him. "Wanna sit down and study with us?" He glides his fingers over her knuckles in the same way he just did to mine. My heart feels like it's crumbling.

She lifts the strap of her beautiful, quilted, black Chanel bag on her shoulder as she steps closer to him. "That's okay." She looks at me again warily.

"Well," she continues. "I just came to grab a book for French. I need to get home and start this paper. Oh, I'm meeting with my father tonight."

I watch as he slides his fingers between hers. "Make sure you get those questions answered for me, okay baby?"

I want to tear her hair out and then run into a corner and cry.

"Of course, Vincent. We're still going to the movies tomorrow night?" She puts her hands in his hair, pushing his gorgeous dark strands back.

"Sure," he says with a smile.

Casually leaning forward, she presses her lips against his. I swallow back a gasp when he pulls out his hands to bring her closer. He's telling me with his body language that they're together. No—they're better than together. They're in love. The most influential couple on campus is sitting in front of me, and it's not just a simple photo on the internet. Their relationship doesn't look like a ruse, and I'm watching it in real time. Everything he just told me goes up in smoke. What's genuine and what's fake? I can't navigate this.

"Vincent!" She gently pushes away from him as if she's trying to calm him down. "Not here!" I've never felt jealousy to this degree in my life as if she just poured salt on a bloody wound.

She turns toward me again, her smile tight. "Why don't you and Tom come to the movies tomorrow. I mean, you are seeing each other, right? So why not all go together?" Her words sound calm, but there's a calculated edge. Is she testing me?

He chuckles casually. "Sure. I'll make sure Tom's free. But, are you free, Eve?" He cocks his head to the side. I have no way out of this right now; I can't think of an excuse fast enough. Although my mind protests, I shrug my shoulders in agreement.

"Good." She opens her bag and checks her phone. "See you later." She walks away from our table, and I feel totally shell-shocked.

I won't look at him; I just can't do it. Seeing her makes the entire thing clear as day. He has a full-on faux relationship with this girl, and she's gorgeous…and she's tall…and she's rich… and she's smart. I've got to get the hell out of here and away from him. I stand up and from the corner of my eye, can see that he's putting his jacket back on.

"Where's your coat? That scarf isn't going to be enough." His voice is concerned, but I'm too upset to give a shit.

I roll my eyes and finally dare to look up at him. "I didn't bring one, Dad." I open the door of the study room and with one step, he's beside me. I refuse to acknowledge his question, even though the truth is that I left my jacket at my mom's, and there's no way in hell I'm going back there again.

We walk outside into the fresh fall air. "I'll just walk back to the quad," I say, still refusing eye contact, taking wider steps so I can get away from him.

He grabs my arm, spinning me around so we're staring at each other. Pulling off his own jacket, he puts it over my shoulders. "I'm driving you back to your dorm." The man doesn't ask; he orders.

"I'm not getting into your car again." I say with as much strength as I can muster, pulling his jacket roughly off my shoulders, handing it back to him.

He steps closer to me, getting in my space. "Take my damn coat and get in the car. You're cold."

"I don't want your jacket!" I yell, shivering from the wind. My hurt is turning me into a crazy person.

"What you just saw wasn't what you thought. You aren't listening to me. I have to keep her off your ass. You're stronger than this, Eve." He moves closer, lowering his voice. "I've got to keep up the façade. If she thinks I have something going on with someone else—if she even smells that I've got feelings for anyone else—she'll go insane. She's just a lie, Eve. She needs everyone to believe we're a couple."

He stands unwavering, a block of stone. I walk to his car, slamming the door shut and throwing his jacket in the back like it's poisonous. I buckle my seatbelt and cross my arms in front of me, anger coming off me in waves. As we drive, my emotions simmer.

We arrive in the quad and he pulls into a parking spot. Leaning forward with one hand resting on the steering wheel, he turns toward me. Why is it that right now, all I want to do is straddle him and kiss him senseless? I want to imprint myself into him so that the entire universe knows he is mine. Not hers, but mine! My mind is fuming, but my body and heart are obsessed.

"Tom will text you about the movies." His mouth is in a tight line.

I let myself out of his car. Even with the tinted windows, I can feel his eyes on me.

CHAPTER 11

VINCENT

I pull over once I'm off campus and dial Tom. After a few rings, he answers.

"Yo." I hear the smile on his face and girls laughing in the background. I raise my head to the roof of the car, annoyed.

"What the fuck are you doing? It's five o'clock on a Monday evening."

"Yeah, so? Everyone isn't as serious as you, motherfucker." The giggling gets louder. "Remember the days you used to actually enjoy pussy?"

I'd reply, but I don't have the energy to engage dumb-as-fuck. "Something's come up. We're going to the movies tomorrow night."

"Cool. Can we see that action flick?"

"Sure. But you've got a date with Eve."

The phone muffles for a second. "Hang on," he says, a question in his voice. I hear some girls complaining in the background and a door slamming shut. "Sorry, dude. Came into the bathroom to hear you better. These girls are seriously insane. Not that I don't enjoy the crazy, if you know what I mean. Anyway, what are you talking about? Why am I going on a date with Eve? I thought she's behind us."

"I was sorting out shit with her in the library. Fifth floor study rooms. Somehow Daniela found her way up there and caught us talking. I lied and told her I was doing you a favor, helping Eve study for Ancient Philosophy."

"Wait." He pauses. "Study. For ancient fucking philosophy? You've got to be kidding me," he scoffs.

"Yeah, study. Because the two of you are hooking up and she needed help. It's actually a pretty hard course." He's silent on the other end, but I can only imagine his red face.

"Fuck no," he spits. "Feed Eve to the wolves for all I fuckin' care. Tell Daniela you fucked her and she's out of your life. The end."

"You will come to this goddamn movie and you will act like you're into her!" I seethe, slamming my hand against the wheel. There's no way I'm letting Daniela hurt Eve…or spread a rumor that she's a whore…or blackball her from a sorority. I know the shit that bitch is capable of, and there's no fuckin' way I'm allowing it. The only way to save Eve from Daniela's wrath is to convince her that nothing has—or ever will—happen between Eve and me."

"Yeah, yeah. I get it. Don't get your panties in a goddamn twist. We'll all go out together. Make it look like she and I are hooking up. And then we're all moving on."

I stay silent, fuming.

"I've got two girls begging to suck my dick right now. I'm not going to sit here on the phone arguing with you. You're a smart man. Use your head. Money is flying into our shit right now faster than a wildfire out in California. We've got the Feds up our asses at the ports. Now isn't the time to ruin this connection with Daniela, brother. I've said it once. I'm saying it again. We're going to the movies and I will make sure Daniela believes that the two of you are nothing. And you wanna know why?" I can hear his hard breaths over the phone. "Because there IS no Vincent and Eve! And then you will delete that girl from your mind so all of us can live in goddamn peace." He hangs up.

I slam my hand against the steering wheel again, cursing.

CHAPTER 12

EVE

Vincent texted me earlier with Tom's number, letting me know Tom will be picking me up for the movies at seven. It's six-thirty and I'm already dressed in a jean skirt and a simple black T-shirt. I was worried I'd be late, and so I overshot my timing. I'd pick up a book, but my nerves are too frayed. And every time I look in the mirror, I find something else about my face that I've recently decided I can't stand. After spending all of my life trying to cover up what I look like, it's weird to all of a sudden give a shit. I know all I have to do is get through this movie, make Daniela believe the truth—that is, there is nothing going on between Vincent and me—and then, move on.

The fact that I'm going against my sister's better judgment has me feeling incredibly guilty. Still, what choice do I have? If I can just get through tonight...

I pull up my phone and see Daniela's newest post on Instagram. She took a selfie of herself in a long mirror, showing off her outfit. Pointy blood-red pumps, light denim that's perfectly distressed with a hole at each knee, a plain white T-shirt tucked in at the front, a long camel sweater, and of course—a gorgeous red-quilted Chanel bag. Twenty-five thousand likes.

Out to the movies with bae tonight. Not sure I'll be able to watch the movie, though… #luckiestgirlalive #hotterthanhollywood #datenight

I stare, unable to take my eyes off the picture. I know he told me this entire thing is for show but it all looks so… perfect! He told me he can't turn from me, now he knows I'm here, but I don't have the type of personality to decipher between social media lies and truth. I can't understand the difference between what my eyes see and what my ears hear from Vincent. I Just *can't*.

My phone pings.

Tom: I'm in the front of the quad.

Me: K

I walk out of the building, breathing in and out. In front of me is a gorgeous white Range Rover, windows darkly tinted.

I open the door, sitting in the passenger seat and buckling up. He's silent next to me. I finally turn to stare at him. He's wearing a black shirt and jeans. Holy crap, he looks scarier than I've ever seen him. Gone is the smiling playboy.

"Let's talk a second."

I exhale loudly, mentally gearing up for what I know won't be a pleasant conversation.

"I know Vincent told you the truth about his relationship with Daniela and the family. And I know you guys had a *thing* going on last year." I stare at him, trying not to show any emotion.

"Tonight is about you and me pretending to be more than friendly. We'll do what we need to do to clean up Vincent's fuck-up yesterday." He stares at me expectantly, waiting for a reply.

"Yes, I know." My voice is full of attitude. I'm furious, and for whatever reason, not afraid to show it.

"Do you also know that I'm going to have to touch you so that she understands you are not a threat to her? I don't want you freaking out—"

"How do you know about that?" I ask accusingly. What has Vincent told him? Internally, I boil.

"I know a lot." The asshole actually smiles, perfect white teeth shining.

"Part of my job description is to have Vincent's back." I blink a few times, understanding that Tom isn't just a typical best friend. He's Borignone mafia—here to support the prince.

"For what it's worth," he continues. "He had no choice but to explain it to me. I mean, shit, after all that went down with Carlos, someone had to clean up that mess, right, Eve?" He says my name with disdain.

"Listen to me." I stare up at the roof of the car, gathering my strength. "I'm not sure what Vincent said or didn't say to you, but it doesn't matter anymore, does it?"

"That's right," he smirks, looking somewhat relieved. "So, I guess you really do understand that whatever you had with Vincent is *finished*. I was worried you had some hope in that pretty little head of yours. But you're too smart. And you'd never want to be the cause of Vincent going to prison, right?" I bristle from his condescending tone.

He pulls out a piece of gum, unwrapping it slowly and sliding it into his mouth.

I blink. "Prison?"

"Daniela's father launders our illegal cash. We can't bury that shit in the fields Pablo Escobar style, can we? Ending things with Daniela means ending business with her daddy. And ending things with her daddy, means the family having dirty cash. The cops will be on our asses in seconds." He chews his gum casually.

"And you've got plans for your own future, don't you? To be the cause of an important man like Vincent Borignone being put away in prison would make a lot of people very. Fucking. Angry." He blows a huge bubble with his gum before it explodes back into his mouth.

I swallow, understanding making my mouth dry up. This is a threat.

"Vincent is family, understand? Nothing comes before that. Not now, and not ever. Especially a piece of ass like yourself."

I clench my teeth. "I heard you, asshole." I stare at him, hard. I may be trying to run from my shitty upbringing, but I also refuse to be a scared little girl, threatened by the big bad mafia boy.

"Look, I'm not trying to hurt you," he says, shrugging a shoulder. "I'll make sure Daniela knows you aren't a threat. I know you've been through a lot—and that for whatever reason—you and Vincent seem to be connected in some really intense way. I'll play along tonight, and then we can all move on." He snaps his gum again and I pull the seat belt down, buckling it over my body. It closes with a *click*.

I raise my head high and with dignity. "Yeah, okay. I get it. No more Vincent or risk putting him in jail. Lie to Daniela. The end," my voice snaps.

"Quick learner." He smirks, facing the wheel. "I see why Vincent is so enthralled. Behind that shy demeanor, you're a damn shark."

We drive for ten minutes down the West Side Highway and finally exit into the city streets. Pulling his car into a private parking lot, the sign reads: $75 per hour. Holy shit! The movie is two plus hours long. I can't believe what he's about to drop in parking costs.

He throws his keys to one of the guys who works there. We finally get to the AMC Theater and through the doors. The place is huge, but I immediately spot him.

Vincent stands by the closest ticket booth to the door, with Daniela by his side. She's staring down at her phone in the same gorgeous outfit that I already saw…thanks to social media. Vincent and I lock eyes for a moment, and then I let my gaze take him in—from his dark jeans to his black hoodie. He's wearing a red and black baseball hat, showcasing his straight roman nose and chiseled jaw. He's scary and huge and sexy as all hell. My legs freeze up, but Tom grabs my hand, ushering me forward.

"Just breathe," he tells me as we walk farther inside. I take his advice and try to relax as I move toward him.

"Yo," Tom starts, pounding his fist with Vincent. Daniela puts up a manicured finger, the universal sign for give me a minute. "I just have to reply to this …" she says to no one in particular as she stares at her phone, furiously typing.

"Eve, I brought your jacket. You forgot it in the library the other day."

My eyes widen as he holds up a coat. What. The. Hell? I'm staring at a beautiful silvery gray puffer jacket, that until this moment, I've never seen before in my life.

"That's not mine," I say under my breath, staring at him in confusion.

"Yes. It's yours. You left it in the library, remember?" His eyes flit over to Daniela, who is still totally oblivious to us; her entire focus is on her phone.

I swallow hard, taking it from his hands. It's exactly what I'd buy if I could afford it. Tears prick my eyes, but I swallow them back.

I squeeze the jacket in my hands before trying it on. It's so soft and light. I zip it closed, tying the belt in a knot around my waist. It's a perfect fit. I touch the hood and my jaw drops to the floor when I feel it, realizing that it's lined in what feels like real fur. I look at Vincent, whose eyes have so much warmth in them that I die a little inside.

I turn to Tom, who looks like he's about to rail. He's squinting at Vincent with a what-the-fuck look on his face.

When Tom sees I'm watching, he looks me up and down, almost resigned. "Look at you. You look like a beautiful little Eskimo." He smiles not unkindly, throwing the hood over my head playfully so I'm practically drowning in warmth and softness.

I pull the hood back down and watch as he looks at Vincent. "Good thing you brought her jacket, man. It's supposed to be a freezing winter." The sarcasm drips off his voice.

"Yeah, it is." Vincent's standing tall with an almost dead-eyed stare when Daniela pops her head up, breaking the tension.

"Hey guys," she says happily, completely having missed the exchange.

"Daniela, you remember Eve?" Tom asks, throwing a heavy arm around my shoulders.

I stare up at her, probably looking as scared and nervous as I feel. She is so tall, staring down at me with a wry grin as if she's trying not to laugh. Insecurity blazes through me.

"Yeah, of course." She raises a perfectly plucked eyebrow. "We met at a party and then the library. While Vincent was tutoring her. Right, baby?" She holds onto Vincent's arm possessively, pursing her lips that somehow look bigger today than the other night.

All of a sudden, her face morphs—as she looks me up and down—with something like shock. "Wait. Where did you get that jacket?"

"Uh, a friend bought it for me." I dart my eyes to the side nervously.

"How is that fucking possible?" she quickly replies. "I've been looking everywhere for that coat in that color, and it's impossible to find! Is it Moncler?" She's fuming. I'm ready to rip it off my back and hand it to her if she'll just calm down and leave me alone.

She puts her hands on the belt of my coat, and I guess it confirms her suspicions. "It doesn't make sense that you have it."

"You're hilarious, Daniela. It's just a fuckin' coat. Go to Bergdorf or whatever and pick one up if you like it so goddamn much."

"You're funny, Vincent," she says mockingly. "I can't just *pick it up* because that color is not available." She moves her hands to her hips, waiting for me to speak.

"Well," I say, my voice quivering. "A friend of mine works at Bergdorf, so I'm sure that's how she managed to get it." I shrug, trying to act as if one of the biggest socialites in New York City isn't about to rip my head off.

"What department?" Daniela counters.

"She's, um, at the hair salon," I say with my head high. The lie twists in my gut, but I do my best to act like the words out of my mouth are truth. And since Janelle does actually work at the salon, I'm sure I could back up my story if need be.

"Whatever." She pulls the phone back from her purse and furiously types, probably ripping her assistant a new one for not getting her this jacket before I did.

Vincent grunts something that sounds like, "The movie's starting soon," and gives the tickets to the bald guy at the ticket booth. He rips them in half, handing the stubs back to each of us as we pass. Vincent chooses seats in the back; no one is behind us.

"Anyone want popcorn?" Vincent asks. I'd love some, but there's no way in hell I'm opening my mouth to say yes. I need to get through the night in one piece.

"Get me a small. No butter. Not even a little bit. Totally plain, okay?"

I'm internally cursing Vincent. He couldn't just buy me a regular jacket from The Gap or something? He had to go and buy me something like this? God, it must have cost a fortune.

Vincent leaves the theater. I think about the crunchy, salty popcorn and sweet fake butter, and my stomach grumbles. Too bad I won't be having any tonight.

Tom takes my hand, lacing his fingers through mine. His hands aren't hard and calloused like Vincent's, but they are still warm. Daniela watches us with a smile on her face. One thing is for sure—Tom is in it to win it. I've got to get my head back in the game and make sure she believes that I'm here for Tom. I snuggle closer into his side.

"Aw! You guys are seriously cute together."

"Thanks," I reply, trying my best to act happy, even though I'm anything but. This movie couldn't start fast enough.

Daniela clicks her tongue. "So, Evelyn, where are you from?"

Tom laughs. "Come on, Daniela. What is this, the inquisition? And her name is Eve, not Evelyn." Tom squeezes my hand in what feels like solidarity.

"Get a life, Tom. I'm trying to make conversation." She smiles, and I feel my palms start to sweat. "If she's your girlfriend, I'm going to be spending lots of time with her, right?"

"She's from the city. Grew up downtown."

"Really? What part?" She seems happy, but a nagging voice in my head reminds me that this is a test.

"Near SoHo," he replies smugly, staring at me as if I'm heaven on earth.

She looks at us skeptically, and I do my best to stare back at Tom as if I couldn't be happier.

"What school did you go to?"

I put my hair behind my ears. "I went to a public school, actually."

"Public?" she says incredulously. "And you still got into school at Columbia? Holy shit, you must be freakin' smart then. Half of these kids got in because their families donate or went here themselves."

"Isn't she something?" Tom says, staring at me with stars in his eyes.

Daniela hums, looking me up and down. "You're so… small. Kind of like a little girl, actually." She's doing that thing again, where she's laughing at me with her eyes. She hasn't said anything so bad, but the energy she's giving off is vile.

"Little girl?" Tom stares at my boobs blatantly and my face heats. "Not in any of the ways it matters, she doesn't. She's definitely…fresh, though, if that's what you're implying." He licks his lips and I'm so embarrassed, I can't bear to look up.

Moments later, the previews begin and the theater darkens. Tom lets go of my palm and I feel relieved. I'm trying to settle into my seat when Vincent returns, handing Tom two drinks.

"Eve," Vincent whispers, handing me a huge popcorn and four different candy boxes. My eyes widen, and I want to jump up and down and scream in excitement. He turns to Daniela next, giving her a small bag.

Movies are expensive as hell, and add in all these treats? It's something I've never been able to afford. When Janelle and I were younger, we'd buy bootleg DVDs from the guys in Chinatown who would bring a camcorder to the movies, record the entire film, and then sell the recording for $1.99 to kids like us. The picture was always a little shaky because no one's hand can stay perfectly straight, and the screen would black out for a minute or two if anyone in the audience stood up to use the bathroom or something. But still, it was as close to a movie-going experience as I could expect.

My gaze moves to Vincent and Daniela, whose hand rubs up and down his leg possessively. His form is rigid. "Ugh, I can't see with this guy in front of me. Can we switch seats, Vincent?" Daniela asks.

They both stand and Danielle squeezes by Vincent, rubbing against his body like a cat before planting herself in his old seat. *Shit*. Vincent is now next to me. His muscular thigh brushes up against mine and I squeeze my legs together, sitting straighter in my chair. He reaches over to me, pulling out boxes of candy from my side. "You feel like chocolate tonight?" I turn to face him and swallow hard, nodding. He opens a box of Reese's Pieces and pours them into my popcorn. "Eat them together; it's the best. Used to eat this as a kid and loved it."

I stare at him dumbly.

"Go on," he says. I put my hands into the popcorn, pulling up a handful of popcorn mixed with the chocolate. The minute I put it all into my mouth, I let out an involuntary moan. "This is beyond good," I tell him with a mouthful. He chuckles and nods at me. "You sure you don't want some?"

He puts his hand in the popcorn, smiling. Bringing up a handful, he puts it into his mouth. "Delicious," he tells me, staring at my mouth. The tension between us is so loud nothing other than him registers.

He leans over me, lifting a drink from the holder next to my seat. "I brought you Cherry Coke and regular. Try them both to see which you want." I bend down, wrapping my lips around the straw. "Cherry," I tell him, my voice a whisper.

"Regular Coke for you," he tells Tom. His eyes don't leave mine.

"Damn. I love the cherry!" Tom complains.

"You want mine?" I immediately ask, turning my head.

"No," Vincent interjects, leaving no room for negotiation. I risk a glance at Daniela, who is thankfully completely focused on her cell phone.

Finally, the movie starts, and I try to relax. Staring at the screen, Vincent leans toward me, shifting his arm so we share an armrest. Then his leg rubs against my leg. I want to concentrate, but it's basically impossible with him this close. I can smell him, all woodsy, soapy, and clean. With each passing minute, he inches closer until his enormous hand is wrapped around my thigh. I clench my teeth, unsure what is going on right now. I shift forward to see Daniela; thankfully she's totally oblivious and still staring at her phone.

Vincent's fingers rove higher on my leg. I keep my head forward, staring at the screen, trying not to pant. My mind and body are engaging in a war right now.

A little higher…

I should make him stop!

His hands are so warm…

His fingers begin to move up and down in a steady rhythm, turning my body into a furnace. What is he doing to me?

I turn toward him, wanting to give him a what-the-fuck-are-you-doing look, but he's still facing the screen. I can see the outline of his dark lashes and the shadows across his sharp cheekbones and scruffy jaw. His face looks even more fierce in this dim light. I never thought it was possible for someone to be so captivating.

His hand roams even higher now, and I lean my head back against the seat, all rational thought disappearing. I'm assaulted by memories of what these fingers can do. Sweat beads on my lower back as his hand drifts upward, centimeter by agonizing centimeter, moving closer to my core. I forgot how possessive he is, but he's showing me right now—loud and clear—that he's the only one in control. Holy shit, but I want to straddle him and then punch him in the face!

I watch from my side-eye as he lifts my Cherry Coke, bringing the straw to his full lips. Tilting his head back slightly, I can see his Adam's apple move with each swallow. It's as if he is completely unaffected. Meanwhile, my panties are damn near soaked. I'm mindless, all rational thought exiting my brain.

Tom stands, walking past all of us to I guess use the bathroom.

Daniela stands up next. "I've gotta make a call."

We turn to each other at the same time; he puts his hands around my ass and lifts me straight into his lap. *Oh my God.* He's so hard. Insistent. Grinding me against him and kissing me like his life depends on it. His tongue drifts down my throat. Before I can even process being on *Vincent*, he moves me back to my chair. Not a moment later, Tom and Daniela both shuffle back to their seats. Can they hear my heavy breathing?

He doesn't touch me for the rest of the movie.

When the film is over, Tom throws an arm around my shoulders. I know I'm supposed to act like we're together, but after that kiss with Vincent, I feel confused and dazed, my heart still beating erratically. We walk out of the theater as a group, and I try not to stumble over my own feet.

Daniela seems relieved; as far as I'm concerned, mission accomplished. Now that I'm no longer an issue, I'm ignorable.

We all say goodbye and Tom drops me off at my dorm. Before I can get out, he locks the door, keeping me within the confines of his car. I turn around, wanting to ask what the hell he's doing when he starts. "Eve. Stay away from Vincent. Our life—and our lifestyle—isn't for a girl like you. Go meet some nice normal guy. You deserve that. That's what Angelo would want, too."

I exhale. For a moment, I forgot that my Angelo is an associate. He may be lowly in their ring, but he's still part of them.

I hear the *pop* of the door unlocking. As I walk to my room, Tom's advice is on repeat in my head. Still, I can't ignore what Vincent does to me—not just in body, but in mind, too. I need to stay away from him because when we're together, the tension is too much to manage. How could I have made out with him like that, and in a public place no less? He makes me completely mindless.

I wish I didn't know who he was behind the mafia man; I wish I had no clue how loving and caring and brilliant he is beneath the hard surface. I sigh, taking off my clothes and gently placing the jacket on my desk chair, and then sliding on an old band T-shirt I got ages ago from the thrift shop.

I know I should give the jacket back, but I don't want to.

Crawling into bed, sleep refuses to come. The thought of tonight being the last time my lips will ever touch Vincent's is killing me inside. I shut my eyes and somehow catch his scent; my heart slows down and I fall asleep, imagining him next to me.

CHAPTER 13

EVE

Sometime later in the evening, I hear a knock. I wake up, startled. Checking my clock, it's after two in the morning. Must be some drunken frat guy. I put my head back on my pillow when the *bang* comes again. I finally stand to get the door, rubbing the sleep from my eyes as I drag myself across the room to open it.

It's Vincent. He steps inside and closes the door, twisting the lock behind him. "What are you doing here?" My voice croaks as my eyes adjust to the man in front of me. I didn't shut the shades when I got home tonight, and the city gives the room a dim glow. My eyes finally acclimate from being awoken and I notice blood trickling down his eyebrow. "Oh my God. You need a doctor!" I press my fingers to my lip in a gut reaction.

He chuckles. "It's nothing a little TLC can't fix." His voice is sure but tired.

I crouch under my bed and pull out a simple first-aid kit that Angelo got for me. Vincent sits at my desk while I grab a washcloth and wet it at the small sink by my door. He sits while I clean off his cuts and cover them with ointment. With him sitting and me standing, we're finally eye to eye.

"Your cheekbone is darkening," I tell him, gently grazing his face with my thumb. "What happened? Was it a fight, or—"

"Tonight, just a fight."

I shake my head, hating how he constantly puts himself in harm's way.

"It's fun for me, that's all. It's one thing in my life that really is that simple. I just do it 'cause I love it. Not for any end." He shrugs and then curses; the movement seems to have caused him pain.

"Did you hurt your ribs?" I help him pull off his shirt, noticing a dark bruise spreading across his side. I want to touch him, but I'm nervous. I gape at his body, my eyes glued to his chiseled muscles.

"Eve," he says my name reverently. I look up. The small towel drops from my grip and onto the floor. His fingers move to my face, slowly grazing my cheek and down to my neck. His touch is gentle but possessive. I shut my eyes, savoring the feeling. I let out a soft moan as he continues to stroke me. "I can't stay away from you. I need you. Don't you need me? I can't be near you and not have you."

CHAPTER 14

VINCENT

Standing up from the chair, I move to sit on her makeshift king-sized bed. She comes next to me, biting the bottom of her lip. She's hesitant, but her face is flushed from my touch.

"My father was in prison." I'm not entirely sure why I'm divulging this information, but something inside of me needs this connection with her. I want to tell her everything. "I was seven at the time. Lived with Tom and his family for eight years while my dad did time."

She hums, letting me know she's listening, her body swaying toward mine as I speak. "My mom died while giving birth to me out on the rez. My dad barely knew her. He actually tried to get gaming off the ground, but the Tribal Council was against having anyone who didn't have Native blood work with them. Even with a Native wife, they didn't accept him. Once I was born, he brought me back to New York. Back to the family. This violence and this life is what I was raised on, Eve."

I shift, bringing her closer to me so that we're touching. I want to pull off her clothes, feel her naked skin on mine. But I have to get this off my chest—

make sure she knows what she's getting with me. It goes against everything I know, but I can't just…take her. She deserves more than that.

"I'm technically perfect for this world. I've got enough self-awareness to understand that I'm built for it physically and mentally. But it's still not what I want. I want out. I want to be free. I can't leave the family in all ways; I understand that. But I'm physically leaving here soon. And when I go, I want you with me. I can't promise a life with a small yellow house and a white picket fence. But I can promise you…maybe a clean trailer out on the rez." She pushes an errant hair from my eyes, a small smile playing on her lips.

"Nothing surrounding us for miles." I raise my eyebrows, looking at her with thoughts of the future in my mind. "I'll buy us a motorcycle and we can spend our nights riding free. I'll work hard and build out the hotel and casino. You can be my lawyer. What do you say? Let's keep this secret, for now. I want the real, Eve. And you're it. I can't wait anymore."

"Vincent." She drops her head onto my chest, wetness moving from her eyes and dampening my skin. I pull her body to mine, wrapping my arms around her small shoulders.

"Say yes, baby." I'm practically groveling, the sound of my voice foreign to me. "Trust me. Trust in me. I have these last few months, and then I'm going out there. You can stay here and we'll do long distance if you want."

She sniffles. "What about the lies? And Tom told me about prison. And you're making it sound so perfect, easy, even. But it isn't, Vincent. And my sister. She—"

"It IS easy. And lockup is always a possibility for me. I'm not going to lie to you. That's the truth. But I'll make it as simple as it can be. We'll be careful. Your sister? She'll understand eventually. Just say yes to me, baby. Say ye—"

She grabs my head and presses her lips to mine, stunning me.

I pull her closer, so every part of me is touching every part of her. I slowly take off her T-shirt. She shudders, completely topless in my arms. Her body is my heaven; I want to worship it.

She moves forward, grabbing the covers to pull them over herself.

"Don't cover yourself from me. Not now. Not ever."

She drops her hands and lets me take my fill of her body with my eyes. God, this girl. Mine. Thank fuck it isn't dark in here; the city lights have me seeing every beautiful inch of her clear skin.

A thought crosses my head—that maybe someone can see through the window. I stand up hesitantly, shutting the blinds with a curse on my lips. It's a reminder that I won't be able to have her openly, and I hate it.

I move back into the bed, pulling her soft and pliant body on top of mine as her small hands frame my face. She leans in, lips to my ear. "Are we really going to do this?" Her voice is a prayer.

I flip her beneath me so she's lying on the bed and shift myself to the bottom, sliding off her underwear with my hands. "Yeah, baby. We are."

Moving back up, I press my hands against her core. She immediately pushes herself toward me. I know what she wants, but I need to drag it out as long as I can. I palm her, feeling wetness straight through her simple cotton underwear. She's soaked.

"Always so ready for me. Fuck. I'm going to give you everything I have tonight, and then some." She's panting now as I shift my hand rhythmically against her. Every single cell in my body is yelling to get closer. To brand her. I want to get so deep inside her I'll become part of her.

She stops for a moment, and my brain registers there's something she wants to say. "What's wrong?"

"Vincent, I—"

All at once, I decide I can't let her continue. I put my thumb over her lips to quiet her. I can tell from her expression she wants to say a million things. She's angry with me for withholding all of this from her last year. She's furious I have this bullshit girlfriend. She's mad I have duties to the family. I stare at her intently. "I know, Eve. I feel all your anger, too. Hang onto me through this, and we'll make it out together. All we need is time."

"How do you read me like this, Vincent?" she asks quietly, grabbing my hair.

"I read you because I listen to you. I listen to your body. I listen to your eyes." I lift her face and start kissing her, bringing the focus back to the moment. Eve is so tiny I can easily move my hands from the tips of her toes up to her entire body. I finally let myself just consume her with my mouth, drinking in her essence.

I take my time sucking on her neck, down her chest and onto her nipples. She doesn't realize what I'm doing, but something primal inside me is forcing me to mark her. She moans from the deep sensation of my mouth sucking on her skin. I know I'm intense, but I can be no one other than myself.

She grips my neck, pulling me down to her. I know she's ready for me. I put two of my fingers into her mouth and she opens wide for me. "Suck."

She does what she's told, twirling her soft tongue and coating my fingers. When I pull them from her lips, she looks at me with nervousness and love. I pause for a moment, swallowing hard and savoring the feeling.

"Eve, I love you. You know that, right?" I couldn't stop the words even if I wanted to.

"Tell me this is real, Vincent." Her voice is a plea.

"This is never-ending."

"Tell me you'll stay safe for me."

"I won't lie to you; I live a dangerous life. You see me here and in school, but I've got duality, remember?"

I slide one wet finger into her core, and she immediately gasps, gripping my shoulders. She's so fucking tight I groan, adding a second finger and curling them up, hitting that spot. I can barely believe that a girl this beautiful has never been touched before. She was made for me. Every second of this moment is mine and mine alone, and I plan on making sure I set a benchmark so damn high, no man on earth could ever compete.

When I look down, her entire body is coated in a light sheen of sweat. Fucking perfect. I finally move up over her. "You still want this? I need to hear it." My voice is a raspy whisper.

"Oh God, Vincent, p-please..." she begs. I slide a pillow underneath her butt, giving me a better angle to enter her.

Eve's skin. Eve's dark hair. Eve's lips, so pouty and beautiful. Eve's nipples, a perfect shade of rose. I see the red splotches all over her chest from my mouth and it spurs me on. Mine.

"Come inside me...don't wait anymore," she begs, hooking her legs around me in an effort to keep me in place. I laugh at her attempt to stop me from moving away. I'm so much bigger than her, there's no way she could physically restrain me. But the truth is with just one word from her, I'd bow at her feet. She's the queen, and I'm nothing but her servant. She doesn't want me to tease her anymore? Her wish is my command.

"I'm clean, but I want to get a condom on until we get you on the pill." I try to move off the bed, but she grips me tightly. "Just a sec, okay?" I kiss her forehead and move off. Pulling out a condom from my wallet, I slide it on. She watches with a wide-eyed stare, looking at my dick with anxiety.

I chuckle. "Don't worry. It'll fit."

"Are you sure? I don't know, Vincent. I don't think that's possible. I mean, I obviously didn't realize before how enormous it is. And I'm so much smaller than you. What if I break?"

I laugh out loud. "I swear it. You were made for me. Nothing will make you feel as good as this. Lay down."

She does as I ask, but I can tell from her body language that she's tightened up. I kiss her lips and neck until she's rolling her body beneath me.

She moves her lips to my ear. "Do it now, Vincent. I'm ready."

I don't listen. Instead, I slide my fingers around her clit, swirling them until she's writhing in pleasure. With a breath, I sink into her heat. It's been a while and I freeze, willing myself to hold back. "You okay?" My voice sounds strangled, even to my own ears.

"Vincent. It's too much—"

"It's okay. Just breathe through it and let your body relax." I smooth the hair away from her face. I know my dick is the first she's ever seen, but if Eve really knew how big I am compared to other guys, she probably would have run away at the sight of it. I don't want to hurt her any more than I have to, so I will myself to be as slow and gentle as possible. Sweat gathers on my forehead, dripping from my head onto her chest.

She grips my shoulders, staring deeply into my eyes as I finally push in all the way. The moment I feel the breakthrough, I have to stop. It feels too good.

I hear her suck in a breath. "It burns, Vincent."

"I know, baby. Keep breathing."

We're all tongues and groans. Never in my life did I kiss like this during sex. Holy shit, but every inch of me is begging for this connection with her. My body is tense from going slow, my movements driving us both to the brink of euphoria. I want to make this good for her. Make it last.

I watch as the electricity enters her bloodstream. "Ohhh," she says on an exhale as if bliss has hit her all at once. She's so close. I track every movement she makes. When her pussy starts to tighten, I think I may pass out. With every thrust, I'm marking her slow and deep. My ribs are aching, but nothing short of a gun to my head would make me stop. Finally, with a groan, I finish. She holds onto me with her legs still wrapped around my waist, and I can sense her unwillingness to let me go.

Pressing another kiss on her shoulder and then her lips, I stand again. After taking care of the condom, I walk to her small closet and pull out a fresh washcloth, wetting it with hot water from her tiny sink. Before getting back into bed, we lock eyes. She's waiting for me with her legs closed, looking at me expectantly. She's unsure what she's supposed to do, and I can't help but laugh.

"Open up for me, baby. I think things may have gotten a little messy." When she opens her thighs, what I see turns me from possessive to wholly insane. I clean her off gently, making sure not to miss a spot.

"You're in me now," she whispers. She has no idea how badly I want that to be true. I want every man who ever sees her to know that she's taken.

I pull her flush against me. "I want to own every single part of you." I grab her waist tightly.

"But you do, Vincent," she replies. "You have me."

The look I see in her eyes? It's more than love. So much is moving between us that I feel high. I shift, kissing her entire body. She's giggling as I find her ticklish spots, nuzzling between her breasts and behind her ear. We kiss and play around in bed and it's so innocent and yet, it's ecstasy. Something I never imagined possible.

Sometime around four in the morning, I stand to leave. She's watching as I dress myself, first with my pants and then sliding on my shirt. My ribs feel like they're on fire, but my heart is too damn happy to care.

"Vincent, don't leave me yet. Why do you need to go?" I hear her distress, but I need to leave before anyone sees me. The truth is, we should have done this at my place in SoHo.

I crouch down by her bedside. "This isn't goodbye, okay? I just don't want anyone to see me leaving here in the morning. I love you." Have words ever felt more natural rolling off my tongue?

She nods her head in understanding.

I lift my hand, scratching the back of my neck. "I'm a selfish fuck, Eve. I couldn't help myself last night. If you're bruised on your neck and chest, don't be afraid, okay? It's just from my mouth. You also might be sore down there. Just take it easy the next few days, yeah?" I know that Eve knows nothing other than me. She was so innocent before I came into her life....*Jesus, forgive me.*

She pushes the sheet down, staring at her skin. "You like marking me." She states it as a fact and she's absolutely right. I do love it. If I could, I'd go back over them now and make the bruises darker. Last longer. Everyone on earth should know she's taken.

I drop to my knees and put my forehead against hers, breathing in her breaths. She lightly pushes me back, forcing eye contact.

"I want to take the risk."

I press our lips together, pulling back for just enough time to get a few words out. "I love you." Kiss. "I fucking love you." Kiss. "So much." I don't let go, even when I taste the salt from her tears. I finally slow us down and push myself back up again.

"Vincent, you're everything to me." Her voice is laced with love, but also pain. "I'm a-afraid, though. I've worked so hard to get here, and—"

"I swear it. I'll never take your future from you." Taking the small gold crucifix off my neck, I push her hair to the side and close the clasp at her nape. Kissing the cross to the center of her throat, I blink into her large brown eyes. Her long lashes open and close, and then somehow, I get myself up and walk out her door.

CHAPTER 15

EVE

I spend my entire day studying. Every time I move my body, I feel where Vincent had been. The reminder heats my blood and makes my heart ache at the same time. I hate the idea of sneaking around. But he's right about one thing; I'd rather have him this way than not at all. He's a risk I'm willing to take. I just have to hang on for the rest of the school year, and then he can publicly break it off with Daniela and we can just be normal. The fact that he's Borignone mafia worries the hell out of me, too. But when he leaves the East Coast, he won't be in the middle of the fire anymore. I believe him. I can handle it.

I hate that I'll be lying to Janelle. While we aren't technically cheating, if anyone else in the world saw us together, they'd assume we were. The idea has my stomach churning. Claire's warning that Daniela would make my life a living hell pounds in my skull, too.

I move my hand to my neck, pressing his necklace against my throat. He loves me. We'll be okay because we have to be. Life can't be so cruel to finally give him to me, and then take him away.

I have an exam in Ancient Philosophy in five days and I need a good grade to do well in the class. I turn back to chapter one, hoping if I read the passages over and over, it'll all become clear to me.

My phone pings.

Claire: Hey girl! Late dinner tonight?

Me: I'm so screwed for my Ancient Phil test. I don't know shit!

Claire: Ugh, it's the hardest class freshman yr. Buckle down!

Me: I'm going to have to pull a few all-nighters studying...

Claire: I wish I could help you but it would be the blind leading the blind. I got a C in that class by the skin of my teeth

Me: I'm not sure what the hell I'm going to do. I got a C- on the last paper and

I need an A on this test if I'm going to pull a decent final grade. Plus, Prof Schlesinger is an a$$hole

Claire: Totally

Claire: OMG! We need to pull a Cher from Clueless and hook him up with some other prof. Maybe if he were getting laid, he wouldn't be such a fucking dickhead!

Me: LMAO!

Me: But all that shit aside, the test! I'm so screwed....

My night passes quietly. Vincent texted me that he was busy tonight with work, which I guess means family stuff. I hope he's okay.

The next morning I'm leaving my chemistry lab when I spot Vincent. We see each other, and I watch as his eyes light up. I want to run to him and say hello when Daniela struts out of a different room, walking directly into his arms and placing a slow kiss on his lips for everyone to see. Her back arches, long hair swishing to the side in perfectly curled tendrils. I struggle for breath while students watch the spectacle.

I shouldn't be dumbfounded, but I am. We're all stargazers in the show titled: *Vincent and Daniela*. Finally, as if the kiss was more like five minutes as opposed to a few seconds, she pulls back. Her hands move up his chest and then into his hair as her lips move. Acid burns straight up from my stomach through my throat. I'm having a physical reaction to them together. I want to run away, but my feet feel as though they're cemented to the floor.

They walk by me.

Vincent ignores my existence.

I drop my head, feeling utterly worthless. I check my cell for the time and notice I'm going to be late for Calculus. I scurry on to my next class, my backpack heavy on my shoulders. I can't think of him now. I have class to attend.

I knew seeing him with her would be like this, but watching it in real time is more painful than I ever imagined. Now that we've had sex, it's as if everything I felt for him before is amplified. For a moment, I imagine if this is how my mom felt when she was the girl on the side for so many men. But then, I push the thought away. Vincent and I aren't like that. We aren't. We really truly aren't.

I run out of the science center and enter the mathematics building. Thankfully, it's my last class of the day. I jog up to the third floor and about to turn the corner when an arm snakes out, pulling me into an empty classroom. I want to scream with fear as the door slams shut behind me. But when I turn around, it's Vincent.

He lifts me up and presses me against the wall. Within minutes, I'm moaning into his mouth, getting lost between his lips and the heat of his body. Pulling back for a second, he stares into my eyes and breathes heavy.

"Hi," he tells me, nuzzling into my neck. I'm in a fog of bliss, but I know that I need to mention what I saw in the halls. If we're going to do this, I can't be afraid to speak up.

"Vincent, I don't like what I saw." I push the words out of my mouth before I can second-guess myself.

"What did you see?" His eyebrows are raised teasingly and I can tell he's trying to play, turn the awkwardness from the hallway into a joke.

"Stop. I'm serious." He doesn't respond, but his eyes turn into slits.

"You know what you saw is what's expected. She needs that public display of affection." His face reddens as if he's trying to stay calm.

"All you ever do is what's expected of you, huh?"

"You're kidding, right?" He lets out a breath, eyes narrowing at me. I swallow hard. "I don't fuck her, Eve. I walk around with her like we're together. That's all there is," he replies angrily.

"Put me down!" I say, struggling to be freed from his arms. He slowly lowers me to the floor and then runs his hands through his thick hair, pulling on the ends as he walks away from me to the other end of the classroom.

"You're unbelievable, Vincent. You're the one who kisses Daniela around the halls, and I'm the crazy one for being mad? How about I have lunch with Jared today?"

He pivots around and in a blink of an eye, he's back in front of me. I forgot how fast he is. The look on his face is terrifying, but I'm not afraid of him. "You touch another man and I will fucking end him. Are we clear? We have gone over this already. Daniela and I have to look like a goddamn couple! You can't get upset every time you see us together. It just won't work."

"I can't stand it. Just—stop touching her!" I stomp my foot on the ground as hysteria rises in my chest.

He lifts me, putting me on a desk and leans into me, his hands on either side of my thighs. "Look at me, Eve. I cannot—under any circumstances—end shit with her right now. I need to keep her happy. This is non-negotiable."

"I know." I hear the whine in my voice but can't help it. I know I'm not being fair but seeing them together guts me.

"Tell me what you want. Talk to me." He moves his hands around my waist, lifting me up and pulling my butt to the edge of the desk, closer to him.

I put my fingers on his lips. "I don't want her touching you here. Your mouth is mine." I move my fingers to his hair. "Or here." I run my fingers through his dark strands, it's wild and sexy as hell.

"I need a haircut," he tells me with smiling eyes.

"No. I love it long like this."

"Then I won't cut it." He presses me to his chest and I let out a long exhale.

I move out of his arms. "Actually, how does Daniela like it?"

"She likes it long too, I think," he grunts.

"In that case, I want you to shave it all off." He laughs out loud and I can't help but giggle. I put my nose into his chest, smelling him. "I love you so much, Vincent. You don't understand."

He lifts my head with his hands, forcing eye contact. "I swear I do." He pulls me against his lips again and I do my best to kiss him with every ounce of myself. "But you can't keep allowing your insecurities to affect you like this. Promise me you aren't going to get upset every time you see us together. I love you and only you."

My eyes inadvertently glance up at the classroom clock. "Oh shit, I'm missing Calculus!"

He shrugs. "Take the skip. You don't need that class anyway."

"Don't be a bad influence on me, Vincent! I need an *A*."

"I wouldn't have taken you out of a class that you were struggling in. You're going to get an *A*. And you're going to get into law school. And all of your dreams will come true."

We breathe each other in, our mouths so close, but not touching.

He lets out a playful growl. "Lips only belong to you. Hair only belongs to you. Dick only belongs to you…"

I slap him in the chest, laughing. I can't help the flush that comes into my cheeks. I love this man.

"Come downtown with me tonight at four. We'll study together."

"Really?"

"Of course."

"I'm doing shitty in Ancient Philosophy. I think you jinxed me that day in the library." I lift my brows.

"It's a good thing I wasn't lying when I said I got an *A* in that class."

"You're kidding me."

"Nope. You have Schlesinger?"

My eyes bug out. "Tell me there is something on this earth you suck at." I raise my head to the ceiling, looking for God. But when I bring my gaze back down to earth, all I'm met with are Vincent's laughing eyes.

"Not the way to speak to your new tutor, Eve."

"Oh hell, no! I'm not letting you tutor me." I pull my hair back with my hands, tying it back with a black tie from my wrist.

He stares at my lips and smirks. "Why not? I'm a good teacher. I have a paper due tomorrow, but I can get it done easily now that my outline is done." I give him a face as if nothing sounds worse. "Don't look too excited, Eve," he deadpans.

I sigh. "All right. Four o'clock?"

"Four o'clock. Don't be late."

"Oh? Or what?" I sass.

"Or you'll get punished." He winks before pulling me in for another kiss.

CHAPTER 16

EVE

"When it comes to Aristotle's Nicomachean Ethics, the most important thing to understand is his explanation of a good life for a human being. Aristotle's approach is a practical one. He sees the one big purpose of human existence is to reach the highest good, which must be both intrinsically valuable and self-sufficient. Remember those prongs."

Vincent is lecturing me right now about Ancient Philosophy. We're sitting together at his dining table, books spread out around us. My feet are bare, resting against his legs.

"Okay, but I don't understand how he understands those two concepts." I bite my bottom lip.

"If something is intrinsically valuable, then it's good in itself and never pursued for the sake of something else. For example, if you study to get an *A*, then studying isn't intrinsically valuable. If you study for the sake of studying in itself, then it is."

"Okay. So like, your underground fights are intrinsically valuable?"

"Exactly." His lips quirk up in a smile.

"Okay, and what about self-sufficient?"

"This means that by itself, it makes life worth living. The good life for Aristotle is a life in which we flourish. Make sure to use that word on the test, yeah? Schlesinger will love it. Anyway, all activity should be directed in such a way to give us that life."

I take a deep breath, feeling like everything is finally clicking. "Okay, Professor Borignone. So, what is the flourishing life?"

"Easy. For Aristotle, it's performing your specific activity, which is distinctive to human beings in general, in a state of excellence."

"Ah hah!" I exclaim happily.

"Let's move to the mean. For Aristotle, the mean is not about balance or moderation. Instead, it's about what is appropriate. Sometimes, it's appropriate to be angry. The mean for Aristotle is one which varies."

"This is where you use practical judgment to know what's right, using deliberation and calculation?"

"Yes!" His smile is blinding.

He takes another huge gulp of water as turns the page of the textbook.

"How do you drink this much and not have to pee every other second?"

He chuckles. "I'm just replenishing. You can't imagine the amount I sweat when I work out. I made the mistake a few years ago of not giving myself enough water and I passed out naked on the locker room floor."

I bite my cheek, shocked at the fact that something that crazy both happened to him, and that he'd tell me about it. Then the image of naked Vincent hits me like a train and I have to bite my cheek to stop myself from cheesing from the visual.

"That mind of yours, always in the gutter, Eve. Didn't your mama teach ya any manners?" His terrible southern drawl has me doubling over in laughter.

Finally, I stop, letting my eyes roam from his neck down to his perfectly cut chest and then back up to his dark eyes.

"Don't look at me like that. I'm trying to help you learn," he says, kissing the top of my head. "Plus, you need a break after yesterday."

I nod my head in agreement, but internally, I'm begging him not to give me a break. Because the truth is, I don't want to wait. Now that I've had him once, I want it again. And again. He pulls back and I let my fingers trace his face. He has two old scars through his right eyebrow. "Where did you get these?"

"Bad boys have scars, Eve." He winks.

"Well, apparently, bad boys aren't very bad these days. They like to be gentle and sweet."

"Gentle and sweet?" Lifting me in his arms, he runs full speed into his bedroom. "Let's see how gentle and sweet I can be, huh?" Throwing me onto his huge bed, he lifts up my shirt and blows into my stomach until I'm crumbling with laughter. The playful side of Vincent is so incredibly unexpected.

His face turns serious as he moves me to the edge of the bed, sinking down on his knees to take my pants off. Next, I raise my arms as he takes my T-shirt over my head.

For whatever reason, I'm feeling braver today than ever before. Maybe it's because I saw him in the hallway with Daniela, and I want to remind him of what he has. Or maybe it's because I'm tired of being the shy girl I used to be.

I stand, removing my bra and underwear. I'm completely nude in front of him. With hooded eyes, he swallows every inch of me with his gaze. Shaking his head as he lifts me up, he carries me into the bathroom. I have no idea why he brought me here, but any questioning thoughts in my head exit my brain as he places me on the marble countertop.

What starts as our mouths moving in a gentle caress quickly becomes frenzied. He's kissing me so deeply that my lips turn numb; I'm mindless from the pleasure. Letting go of my mouth, he lowers his head, licking and sucking on my nipples, moving from one side to the next.

"You like that, baby?" All I can do is whimper. My body is humming, core pulsing with need. Releasing one breast with a pop, I feel cold air take the place of where his hot mouth was. I open my eyes, wondering where he's gone. And why—of all places—he brought me to the bathroom when we were just in a perfectly warm and comfortable bed.

The flat of his tongue takes a long and deep sweep out of my center and my body jackknifes with surprise. Holding my legs open with both of his hands, he starts out slowly, taking his time. "You taste like fucking heaven, Eve. Better than I ever dreamed."

Any embarrassment I may have had disappeared with his words. It isn't long until my moans grow loud. I'm shaking and can't stop. Sweat beads between my breasts, the heat of his mouth consuming me. My body is undulating, completely out of control. Grabbing my hips with his enormous hands, he keeps me secured to the earth as he sucks and hums. Just as I'm climbing toward a high, I feel his calloused fingers trailing down my body, and pressing where his mouth is sucking. I'm seeing stars. All I can do is grab onto his shoulders as I ride out the most euphoric feeling of my life.

"I can't possibly handle anything more," I say to myself. But he brings his tongue back inside me, not stopping until he sucks every morsel of pleasure from me. With glazed-over eyes, I watch as he kisses back up my body. The warmth of his lips feels like heaven and I want to curl into a ball and sleep for eternity.

The thought that Vincent may end up running the biggest mafia in the country passes through my head. The photos I've seen with him and his Daniela enter my mind. And just like that, straight behind the most pleasurable experience of my life, I start to cry.

"Eve? You're crying?"

I nod my head, unable to control the torrent of feeling.

"I'm that good, yeah?" My tears stop and I stare at him for his asshole remark when a smile spreads across his handsome face. He's...joking!

"Oh, you!" I exclaim, laughter mingling with staccato breaths.

"Tell me. Talk to me."

"It's just, Daniela. And your family. And my sister would go insane if she knew, and I feel so guilty..."

"We're together now. I'm going to find a way out of this shit with Daniela. We just have to be patient. Can't you be patient for me?" He's talking, but I only cry harder, body wracked with tremors.

My mind registers Vincent is fully dressed. Meanwhile, I'm sitting here on a bathroom counter, completely nude with my huge boobs—that are way too big on my small frame—out in the open. I cover myself up with my arms. The strong girl from a few minutes ago is gone, and, in her place, sits a nervous nineteen-year-old.

He uses his hands to lift my chin. "I think you need to hear it straight. I'm a man with lots of needs, and I want it all from you. Do not cower in front of me. Ever. You're stronger than that. I know you've been through a lot, but you aren't weak." His voice is firm.

Every cell inside me wants to open up to him. I don't want to hide. I want to give him everything. I move my arms away from my body, baring myself to him.

"There we go." His voice comes out with a sigh.

I pull back, staring at each part of his face in isolation. His gorgeous chin and chiseled jaw. His sensual lips. His straight Roman nose and wide cheekbones, giving his face a perfect symmetry. My eyes move up to his dark eyes that see straight through me. In his gaze lives the most beautiful version of myself. It's where my strength lives. It's where I'm not a poor hood rat, but an intelligent woman who can achieve her dreams. The ideal version of myself lives within Vincent.

"You are everything right in my life. Understand?" His voice is deep and full of love.

Leaning his forehead against mine, he breathes heavily. Then he wraps me up in his arms, lifting me with one arm and turning on the shower with the other. When the water is warm enough, he places me into the spray.

From behind the glass, I watch as he takes off his clothes. I lean against the door to stabilize myself. His broad shoulders and muscular arms are incredibly sexy. His chest is sprinkled with some dark hair. My eyes move downward and I literally gasp, shocked again at how huge he is. There's no way in hell he's normal. The combination of seeing him naked after what he just did to me makes my legs weak.

When he finally joins me, my breath hitches. Our eyes lock as he lifts me up again in his arms, my hands finding the back of his hair. Steam billows around us as he presses me against the cold marble wall. I'm searching for answers within his kiss as we claim each other with wet mouths and water-slicked bodies. My soft body rocks against his hard, asking for more. More. More. "Please," I beg. "I want you."

He pulls away from my lips and looks at me, pushing my wet hair out of my face. "I know what you want. But I don't want to hurt you. It's too soon after yesterday."

"No. Now. I need this now. Want this now." His eyes darken, turning almost black.

"I'd kill for you. To make you a part of me, I'd do anything. I'm a selfish man, Eve. I'll never let you leave me."

With my legs wrapped around his waist, he enters me in one push.

I can feel him deeper than I ever thought possible—his dick pulsing and growing larger inside me. My throat aches from how loud I'm moaning. "Let me hear you. Let me hear how badly you want it." One of his hands is splayed on the tile behind me; the other grips my ass.

When I feel myself building up for another orgasm, he holds me tight against his chest. I unravel right into his arms. Not a moment later, it's his turn. He pulls out before he can finish inside of me.

Eventually, he lowers me to the ground, dragging my naked body down his. Turning me around, he squeezes some shampoo into his fingers and washes my hair. The act is so gentle and loving; I have to put my hands on the wall to keep from falling. After my hair is clean, he drops himself down onto one knee, turning my body toward him. When he lifts up my right foot, I lean my hands on his massive shoulders. He soaps me from the tips of my toes up my thigh toward my center. I gasp as his hands move upward, gently cleaning a place only he has ever been. When he's done with my lower half, he rubs his soapy calloused hands over my breasts and down the sides of my body. Then he turns me around and soaps my entire back, gently massaging me. When he's done washing me, he cleans himself. I can only stare in wonder as he lathers, raising his arms up one at a time to clear away the soapy suds.

Turning off the shower, he steps out before me to get fresh towels. He places one around his trim waist and then opens the shower door, wrapping me up in a second. I've never had someone take care of me like this. I'm trying not to cry again, although this time it would be out of sheer happiness. Holding my hand, and gently walking us back into his bed, I move to my side as he joins me.

We're face to face, lying together all cozy, wrapped up in his covers. He's smiling and my heart is soaring. "So, you think you'll ace this test? You need philosophy for law. Make sure to take Logic next semester with Professor Weiss." I brush my nose against his, breathing in his breaths, taking him in. I slide my legs between his, wanting our bodies to touch in every possible way.

I press my lips together. "You know I've watched like, every single *Law and Order* episode in history. I thought that one day I'd be prosecuting gang members." We start chuckling and before I know it, we're laughing so hard we're wheezing. When I let out my signature snort, his laughter intensifies.

We calm down and our eyes turn serious. "Vincent. How many weeks until you leave?" I stare at his chest, swallowing hard.

"Sixteen." I finally look back up at him again and he nods his head.

"What's it like out on the rez? I heard it's pretty crazy out there. Like, third-world in some parts, right?" I want to discuss this with him, but I also don't want to say something wrong. I'm hanging onto his every word, just hoping he tells me everything.

"You wouldn't believe this, but there isn't any water there. People literally drive their trucks an hour back and forth just to get fresh water to drink. I mean sure, there are watering points, which are just hoses in towns bordering the rez. But there's still no groundwork or infrastructure to bring water directly to people's homes. There are some windmills and wooden buildings which house wells, but they are totally contaminated. And people drink from that."

His eyes are registering something like distress. I can tell he's passionate about this.

"So, yeah. I want to get back out there. A casino complex on the lands would change the face of tribal economics. And if I can get in there and make that difference, I'll do it even if I have to let the waters run red for a while. One of my main goals is to find a way to bring that infrastructure onto the rez. I'm sure Nevada would be willing to help out if I gave them a cut of profits. Tribes in other states have worked out deals like that."

"Sounds like some plan, Vincent." I stare at him in absolute awe.

"Don't look at me like that. I haven't done anything yet." His face is serious, and for a moment, I get a flash of Vincent ten years from now. He's already so powerful and magnetizing. This man is going to be someone important one day; I can just feel it.

"Yeah, but you will. It's obvious that you'll do this. People do incredible things all the time. Why shouldn't it be you?"

"You're looking at me right now like I'm a savior. But if you know half the shit I've done..." He lets out a breath. "I'm not a stranger to the life, Eve. The corruption out on the rez and what I'll be doing to get the Tribal Council to go into business with us will be extreme. I'm not going to lie to you and tell you there won't be violence at first."

"I know. But, sometimes wars have to be fought for the betterment of the people, right?"

His gaze turns reverent as he moves his hands around my entire face, tracing my eyebrows and down the straight slope of my nose with his thumbs. He runs his middle finger around my lips and I snake my tongue out, trying to lick his finger. He smiles but continues up my cheekbones and down my ears.

"Jesus, you're so beautiful." His hands are on my face, palms against my cheeks and then down, pressing the cross against my chest.

"Vincent, you're everything," I tell him, wanting to cry again. It's an emotional onslaught.

"Eve, you're perfect." My smile is so huge I feel my eyes crinkle in the corners. "I carry your heart. I carry it in my heart." His face must mirror mine because all I see in his eyes is love.

"Quoting e. e. cummings?"

"You know it." He laughs.

"Vincent, I was thinking—"

"Thinking?" he says the word with distaste and I slap his shoulder, holding back a laugh. He's obviously joking with me, and I love it.

"So, I was thinking…maybe I should transfer to a school in Nevada. I don't want to be far from you." I swallow hard, nervous to be mentioning this. But the truth is, the idea of being across the country from Vincent seems like torture. I'm sure I can still get a great education at another school.

"You're at one of the best colleges in the country right now. I'm not taking that away from you."

"No." I vehemently shake my head. "I don't want to be across the country from you. What if I go to California or find somewhere on the West Coast? I can find a great school out there. We'll still be separated, but at least I won't be all the way on the East Coast while you're out on the West." My voice is small but hopeful.

He takes a few breaths before nodding his assent.

Somewhere inside me, I realize if I thought I loved him before, this man is now imprinted within of me. All of my emotions buzz from the top of my skin down into my bones. I wonder if he can feel it.

He runs his hands along my arms until he reaches the curve in my sides. We're staring at each other in silence, the time passing. He pulls the covers over us again, kissing every inch of my body.

We're in so deep. I nuzzle into the palm of his warm hand.

"We're forever. I'll never stop loving you." His voice is a whisper.

He's on me again. I'm aching but saying *no* to Vincent feels like sacrilege. Instead of entering me this time, he kisses down my entire body and stops right where I wished he would. Oh, this man's mouth.

Time moves like a smooth current until we're soaked with sex and bliss. "Want to watch some TV?" He's smiling wide, playful, and sexy as hell.

I hand him the remote from the side table and he switches the television on. He props himself up on a few pillows against the headboard and I rest my head on his chest. Scanning some movie titles, we settle on an action-packed movie with a little romance.

I touch my hair with my hands and feel the frizz. He turns to me and laughs as I sit up, trying to tame my hair with a braid. Before I can finish, he pulls me back down and undoes my hair. He puts his hands through the strands. "Don't touch it."

We're staring at each other again, all lines of communication open. I want to climb inside him right now.

I wake in the middle of the night curled into his body. It takes me a moment to realize where I am. I put my nose to his side and breathe him in. I want to fall back asleep but can't stop twisting and turning—going back and forth in my head about whether or not this will actually work out. I want our love to win. I want it to be enough.

Sometime around four in the morning, my thoughts turn to fire as Janelle's words flash back to me. Has he killed people? *Of course he has*, a nagging voice in my head replies. Is he going to end up in prison? What if his dad never lets him leave? My heart pounds.

When he wakes, he turns over and takes a look at his watch. Moving toward me, he lets out a warm smile. I want to melt back into him, but I can't help the feeling of doom that's curling around my chest.

CHAPTER 17

EVE

Three months later

I finally finished my last midterm exam—Spring break has officially begun. I'm not planning on leaving campus, though. This is my home now. Vincent and I have been amazing. Ever since we got together, we've spent almost every night downtown in SoHo at his apartment. He brings me with him twice a week to work out, too. It turns out I love mixed martial arts, and I'm pretty good at it. His trainer, Sergey, is awesome, and I've already gotten much stronger.

The only times we're separated are when we're in class, or if he has family business to attend. I know he sneaks moments in with Daniela for the camera, but I try to pretend those times don't exist. I've even gotten off social media. Watching them together, even if it's fake, is too much for me to handle.

Janelle is over tonight, celebrating the end of midterms. We're planning on hanging out in my dorm first, and maybe going out to a bar later. We haven't seen each other as much as we wish we did, but the truth is that between school and sneaking around with Vincent, my time is limited. I know eventually I need to fess up and tell her about what's going on. But I want to push that conversation as far into the future as I can. She just wouldn't understand, and I'm worried about losing her. Her threats still hang heavy in my heart.

Tonight, we're playing some Drake on her phone and drinking wine when I hear a knock.

I open the door to see Claire decked out in a tight black dress and black ankle booties. Her hand is wrapped around a magnum of wine.

"Eve," she squeals, hugging me with her free hand.

"Hey, babe!" I'm surprised but excited to see her.

"I've been texting you nonstop and you weren't answering, so I figured I'd just stop over."

She walks into my room, eyes widening at my sister. "Tell me you're Janelle." She drops the wine bottle on the table and then throws her arms around Janelle as if they've known each other forever.

They both laugh. "That's me. I've heard so much about you."

"Oh my God, I love your hair!" Claire starts.

"You've gotta come by my salon and let me highlight you." Janelle puts her hands through Claire's locks in that expert way, lifting up different pieces and analyzing her color.

"Yes! I want to go blonder. Maybe a few lighter pieces around my face, you know?"

"Absolutely. I can do it for you. Call the salon at Bergdorf."

"How amazing that you work there? When Eve told me, I freaked. Do you do all the celebs and stuff?"

"Yeah, I do a lot of them actually."

Claire turns to me as she takes her jacket off. "Get dressed, ladies. We're going to a club tonight."

"Wait, what?" I ask.

"You heard me." She pulls out a wine opener from her huge purse and proceeds to uncork the bottle. "We've all been studying like crazy, and finals are now over, so you have no excuse. We're going out to celebrate—everyone is going. See this outfit?" She stands tall, gesturing to herself. "I've got to be seen!" She pulls out the cork and reaches into her bag, taking out a plastic wine glass.

I laugh out loud. "Tell me there's a puppy in your bag, and I'll consider it."

"There's a horse in here, not a puppy!" We all laugh.

"We gotta get dressed if we're goin' out!" Janelle says excitedly. She moves to my closet, searching for clothes when she takes out a black halter-top that I conveniently took from her side of the closet before we moved out. "You little bitch!" she exclaims. "I was searching for this top everywhere!" She pulls off her T-shirt and slides it on.

I'm watching Janelle flit around getting herself glamorous, while Claire pours herself wine and kicks off her shoes. All of a sudden, they seem to realize that I'm not getting dressed.

In a blink, they huddle around me like I'm Cinderella, forcing on different outfits until they decide on a tight red dress, also conveniently taken by me from Janelle's side of the closet. I want to argue that I don't want to wear something so flashy, but another part of me wants to experiment, too.

Janelle immediately gets to work on my hair and makeup while Claire tops off my wine. When she's done, I stare in the mirror, stunned. I still look like me, but much older and a hell of a lot sexier. I'm bronzed, highlighted, and my lips are lined and filled to perfection.

Claire chokes on her wine. "You are a genius, Janelle. I mean, Eve is beautiful. But this takes her to a whole other level." Claire turns back to me. "You're definitely hooking up tonight!"

Claire's phone pings and she stares down to read the text. "It's Tom. He's also going to be at the club!"

"I guess we're clubbing tonight," Janelle says happily in a singsong voice, flipping her hair a few times. "Who's Tom?"

"He's a guy I used to hook up with. Oh shit." Claire nervously puts her fingers to her lips. "I wonder if Vincent is coming."

Janelle squints her eyes and my heart pounds.

"Vincent and Tom are sort of like a package deal," Claire explains. "They're both hot, but Vincent is like, off the damn charts. I'm sure Eve told you about him, right?" Her eyes flit between us as Janelle's gaze liquefies into fury.

"Wait. You mean, Vincent *Borignone*?" She purses her lips, waiting for the ball to drop. I hold my breath.

"Yup," Claire supplies easily. "The one and only."

"Oh, yes. Eve told me all. About. Him." She punctuates every word, seemingly trying to keep herself calm.

"I'm gonna use the bathroom before we go." I stand abruptly and run down the hall, with my phone in hand.

Running into the stall, I shoot out a text to Vincent.

Me: Hey. My plans changed. Claire came over and wants us to all go out. Heard you're coming?

Vincent: I'll be there. I know I can't touch, but I'll be watching

Me: I like that. Janelle is with us, too

Vincent: Cool

Me: She hates you, by the way

Vincent: One day she'll get over it. When we're together and all this shit is behind us

Me: I can't wait…

Vincent: Love you baby

Me: Love you too

We all walk together out of the dorms when Claire's phone rings. She answers and immediately begins chatting about tonight's plans. Janelle squeezes my hand and I turn to her.

"I'm going to nail that man's balls to the wall tonight for what he did to you last year!"

All of a sudden, Janelle pauses, eyes widen as she stares at my jacket. "Eve. Tell me where you got that coat."

"Janelle, stop it," I hiss, turning my eyes to Claire. Thankfully, she's too busy on her phone to notice our conversation.

"Oh my God. Tell me you did what you promised. Tell me you aren't seeing him."

"Now isn't the time to explain. There's so much happening—" I bite my cheek and look down.

"You had sex with him, didn't you? How long has this been going on?" Her eyes are murderous. "You swore to me you'd stay away."

I want to lie, but I can't. Instead, I keep my mouth shut. Claire hangs up the phone and tells us Tom is sending a car to pick us up at the dorm.

"How lucky are you two to have friends who are so well connected?" The sarcasm drips from her voice.

Claire moves her gaze between Janelle and me. "Why do I get the feeling something is going on? Is this about Vincent?"

Janelle puts a hand on her hip and stares at me pointedly.

"No, nothing is about him. We're just friends is all."

Claire's jaw drops. "Do you have a death wish or something, Eve? If Daniela ever finds out—"

"Exactly!" Janelle exclaims.

My face must be red; I can feel the heat traveling through my veins. "He has a lot going on, a-and..." My words are coming out in stutters; I'm not prepared for this.

They both stare at me unhappily. "It's your life. But don't say we didn't warn you." Claire shakes her head from side to side.

I look down when Janelle takes my hand. "Tonight, let's have fun. You deserve it after all your hard work. I just wish you'd use your brain and choose someone else. He's—"

"Let's just leave, okay?" I swallow hard, knowing how lucky I am that Janelle didn't fulfill her promise of never speaking to me again. She's not simply my sister or my best friend. In so many ways, she's truly my other half.

A large black Escalade shows up right in front of my dorm. The driver opens the door, and we all climb inside.

Stepping into the club, a beefy-looking guy walks us straight to a table on the right side of the dance floor.

I see Tom first; Claire must not have told him that she was with me, because he looks pretty mad I'm here. Trying to ignore him, I walk over to where Claire's friends are sitting. Everyone is in a great mood, celebrating the end of finals. I spot Vincent, sitting in a dark corner with his hat pulled down low. Even though it isn't easy to see him, I can feel his gaze on me. I force my feet not to run to him.

Looking around, I wonder if Daniela will show up tonight. I silently pray she is sick with the flu and stuck in bed, puking with a raging fever while her little white dog chomps on her favorite red-quilted Chanel bag. I chuckle at my evil musings. But deep down, I know she always is sure to be where Vincent's at in public.

Claire hands Janelle and me shot glasses full of Bacardi. I feel his eyes on me as I swallow it down. I see him from my side eye, nodding at me; wordlessly letting me know he's watching.

Claire and Janelle grab my hands and bring me to the dance floor. We grind up against each other as heat pulses inside my veins. I watch Vincent lean forward, elbows resting on his knees. I incinerate from his stare.

Claire bends down, putting her lips to my ear. "Holy shit, Eve. Vincent is staring right at you!" Her voice is nervous but excited.

My heart skips as Vincent stands up, seemingly walking toward me. My heart pounds so loudly, I'm sure the entire club can hear it. My eyes lock on his. I want him so bad in this moment, I could scream.

I hear a loud squeal before I see her. Turning toward the sound, I watch as Daniela glides in and grabs Vincent's shirt. Moving up to her tiptoes, she kisses him while their friends whistle at their display. Her tongue slides into his mouth and my heart drops into my stomach. I watch as Janelle surveys the scene. She's shaking her head angrily. I squeeze her hand, yelling into her ear, "Let's get another shot."

We walk to our table where I find a bottle of tequila sitting on ice. I pick it up and pour us four. I shoot two drinks, watching as Daniela whispers something to Vincent. I'm staring at them so hard I barely feel the burn of the liquor. She moves onto his lap as if it's her rightful spot, removing the hat from his head.

My eyes bug out as she screams, "You shaved your head?" Her shriek has the table craning their heads toward her. Vincent's hair is buzzed in a military style, and he looks like a total sexy bad ass.

He turns to me for a moment and winks. God, he looks gorgeous like this. With his chiseled face and sharp jaw, he's sin. I can't stop the smile spreading across my face.

When Daniela notices everyone watching her, she flips her shiny red hair to the side, composing herself. Smiling confidently, she possessively rubs a hand against his head, pulling him closer to her. Every cell in my body is screaming at her to stop. Didn't he swear that his body is mine? Mine! My rational mind knows this isn't real, but anger blurs all my senses. I want to yell like a maniac. I want to claw her eyes out!

Vincent is turning me into a monster.

All I can see in this moment is Daniela.

Daniela's perfect hair.

Daniela's gorgeous face.

Daniela's model-perfect outfit. Touching my tight red dress, I realize how cheap I must look compared to her. She is high-end-designer, and I'm the Chinatown copy. Insecurity blazes through me. I'm a wooden house and her perfection is like lighter fluid, her beauty and wealth the matches.

I turn to find Claire is next to me. I put my hand on her arm, desperately needing reassurance. "Do I look like shit? Is my hair frizzing?"

She stumbles back a bit but then rights herself, holding onto me for support and giggling drunkenly. "Eve, you might be the most gorgeous girl I've ever seen!" She hiccups while I look at her with hope. In one moment, Daniela managed to steamroll my self-esteem. "Everyone has been talking about you since you came to school. You're by far the prettiest girl in this club and I don't know what the hell is going on with Vincent, but he's obviously ob-sessed with you."

Her eyes move behind me for a moment. "Oh. Shit. Don't turn around, but Vincent's staring at you and like, isn't even blinking."

"Is Daniela still sitting on his lap?" I need Claire to be my eyes.

"The fucked-up thing is that yes, she is. She's on him, but his eyes are only on you. Oh no, she's—"

Hands grip my shoulders, spinning me around. It's Daniela, and her smile is so fake it sends an actual shiver down my spine. "Hi, sweetie!" she says, throwing her arms around me as if we're best friends. Taking my hand, she practically drags me to a corner of the club, away from prying eyes.

The corner is dark. She drops my hand as if it's diseased. "I see now that you have a little crush on MY Vincent. You like to look at what isn't yours, huh? Did you fuck Tom just to get closer to him?" My eyes widen with her accusation, tongue frozen in my mouth from fear.

"Wait a minute." Her smile turns lethal as her face darkens, as if she's realizing something for the very first time. "Vincent fucked you already, didn't he?" She rolls her eyes before shrugging. "That's Vincent. He's wild in bed; needs a lot to keep him satisfied. Do you get nice and dirty for him, how he likes? There are things he wouldn't dare do to me. I'm too classy for that."

She lets her eyes rove from my toes up to my face. "But you?" She chuckles, pressing a French-manicured nail up to her lips. "I can see how a girl like you would be up for anything. All desperate and cheap, giving it up so easily and willing to do anything he wants." My stomach drops, pain filling the space between my lungs.

"You see, no matter who he fucks, I'm the one he's going to show up with in public. I satisfy him in a way you never could. Meanwhile, you spread your legs for just a moment with him. Girls like you are a fucking dime a dozen," she sneers.

Flipping her hair to the side, she continues, "My rightful spot is next to him, and he wouldn't want it any other way. He and I go together perfectly. And your spot? Your spot is to be his *whore*. Because that's all you'll ever be to Vincent."

Stepping backward, she puts a smile back on her face before turning on a high heel. I try to focus on the world around, but it's spinning. Somehow,

Janelle finds me, bringing me back onto the dance floor. I see Vincent and Daniela again. But this time, it's Daniela making eye contact with me as she kisses him, probably moaning into his mouth. He pushes her off, and I see his lips move. It looks like he's saying "enough," but I can't be sure.

Strobe lights flash, creating shadows on the walls around. I try to go with it, letting the music take me away.

The competitive part of me rears its head. I want him to wish it was me on his lap, not her! I want him to picture my lips on his, not hers! Even though the music is going fast and my head is spinning from the liquor, I consciously slow my pace. All I can process from my conversation with Daniela is that she thinks I'm no one. She thinks I'm just trash. Well, fuck her! That man is mine!

Licking my lips, I stare at Vincent. Moving my body seductively, I try to communicate with my movements how badly I want him. I shut my eyes and throw my head back, letting my hair drape down my back. I know how much he likes when my hair is wild like this. I want him to read my gestures…to understand that I need him now. I need him inside me. Everywhere, all at once. In the back of my mind, I realize that Daniela is willing to throw down, and fighting her is a really bad idea. But in my drunken haze, I couldn't care less about anything or anyone else. I want him to prove to me that I'm the only one.

As I dance, the entire scenario plays out in my head. I picture him coming up behind me, his hands pressing me against his hard body. I imagine him taking my hand, pulling me into the bathroom. Pressing me up against the stall, kissing me, and turning me mindless. He'd lift up my dress and give me what I've been both consciously and subconsciously asking for since the moment I met him.

I feel a man come up behind me. Instead of walking away from him, I press myself to his front, feeling him harden. I screw my eyes shut, imagining that it's Vincent. This guy is exactly what I need right now: a prop. I move against him, opening my eyes for a moment to see if Vincent is watching me. His jaw is ticking; I can practically see his teeth grinding together. Is he angry? I want him mad as hell. I want him to realize how it feels to see me with someone else. He used to have sex with that vile bitch, and it infuriates me. Everyone on earth believes they belong together, and it makes me sick. I'm angry at her for saying that shit to me, but I'm livid at him for putting me in this position. I hate being hidden. I hate being ignored. It's not fair!

He's got a drink in his hand and I watch as he brings it up to his full lips. He tips the drink into his mouth and I watch him swallow. I close my eyes again, slightly moaning, dancing against this random body.

When I finally re-open my eyes, Vincent is gone. I feel my stomach drop as I look around. Did he get so mad that he left with Daniela? What time is it? I need my phone. Where is my bag? Anxiety and alcohol are wreaking havoc on my insides. When the guy tries to pull me to him, I shake him off me, quickly running to the table.

Claire is sitting on Tom's lap, whispering in his ear. I interrupt them. "Claire, did you see Vincent?" I feel myself sway, my voice raspy and eyes dry. Even in my drunkenness, I can see that she's looking at me with pity. A scenario becomes clear in my foggy mind. It's everything I just imagined—except instead of me with Vincent in the bathroom—it's Daniela. Daniela is against the wall. Vincent's lips are on HER neck. She's moaning. Everyone knows they are in there. I'm stuck out here, the idiot. He's fucking her. She's better for him than me.

I'm completely messed up, engaging in this weird triangle I'm not equipped to handle.

Janelle moves behind me. "I think you should go home. You've had too much drink. Let me get us a cab."

I continue to look around the room. Where is he? I need Vincent. The tears well up in my eyes. Is he mad at me?

Tom stands, saying something to Janelle. Not a moment later, he's grabbing my arm. "Let's go, Eve. Your night is over."

"What the hell, Tom?" I'm furious as he hustles me forward, not giving me a chance to even say goodbye. I'm teetering on my heels as Tom drags me out of the club.

Right outside, a black Escalade stands with its engine running. Tom opens the car door, pushing me in and throwing my purse behind me, like used trash.

"Tom?" I'm confused, my brain muddled. He slams the door shut. Looking at the driver in front, it dawns on me this is the same car and driver that picked us up tonight.

The door reopens and Vincent jumps in the back. Fuming. I should be afraid of his intensity, but instead, I feel my own anger bubbling up—and my want.

"You're lucky I was there," he sneers. "You can't just grind against random guys at clubs. You know what you're asking for, right?" His voice is condescending and dripping with antagonism.

"Yeah?" I sass. "Well, I'm just trash, anyway. The girl who spreads her legs for nothing while you go out with the fancy girl in public?" The bitterness in my voice surprises me.

He gets closer, lowering his voice to a dark whisper. "You think I treat you like garbage, huh?" My eyes widen with anxiety. This isn't my Vincent. This is Vincent Borignone.

I press myself against the door, trying to get some distance when he reaches over me to buckle my seatbelt. "Don't touch me!" I shriek. In an instant, his huge hand is around my throat. I freeze. He's not squeezing or hurting me, but I know that he could if he wanted to, and that thought alone is enough to immobilize me.

His face is hard as stone. "You want to know what being treated like a whore feels like, Eve? Should I make you suck my dick right now and then throw you out of the car? Should I hand you my black AmEx and tell you to go shopping for a day before I share you with my friends?"

I can't breathe. I blink, salt water coating my face. I'm crying.

"I'm mad as FUCK right now!" He slams his hand against the seat in front of him. "You think you can walk around a club, touching a man who isn't me?" His voice echoes around the car.

He's scaring the shit out of me and turning me on like I didn't know was possible. My body is acting completely out of control and I have no wherewithal to rein myself in. He lets his hands roam down my chest and onto my legs, lifting my dress higher and caressing my upper thighs with his fingertips. My panties are instantly soaked. My body knows what his hands can do, and my legs immediately part for him.

"You wanted to make me jealous with that fucking guy? You got your wish, baby." His hands rove higher, calloused thumb skimming the edges my underwear. *Oh, God.* I tilt my pelvis up as I lean back into the seat.

The moment I shut my eyes, his body heat disappears. I sit up, noticing that he's no longer near me. It feels as if he's punishing me. Even though my mind is telling me not to, I move closer to him.

"Vincent, I'm sorry, okay? I hated seeing you guys together. Why did she even show up? She t-told me how you like to be dirty. Told me that I'm nothing." I'm shuddering, feeling cold and hot and nauseated. Is he going to leave me because I danced with someone else? I'd die if he leaves me. My tears fall harder down my face.

He turns back to me, his eyes frigid. "What else did she say to you?"

"She told me that I'm not the first, but she'll always be the only. She told me…she told me…you've been with a gazillion girls! But sh-she's the only one who matters. She's the wife; I'm cheap, and I'm the whore."

He pulls me onto his lap, shushing me while I ugly cry. Somehow, I fall asleep in his arms.

Before I know it, my door opens. I wake up seeing Vincent crouched down onto the pavement, angling my body toward him. Before I can ask him what he's doing, he pulls off my high heels. "Ahh!" I gasp as they drop off my feet.

"Oh, it hurts," I moan. He squeezes my arches with his thumbs and I cringe from the pleasure and pain. Lifting me up in his arms, I immediately wrap my legs around his waist and rest my head on his shoulder. He walks me up the flights of stairs to my dorm room as if I weigh nothing at all, putting his hands into my bag to pull out my keys.

Dropping my face into his neck, I take a deep inhale. "You smell so good, Vincent. I want to smell you forever. Tell me we're forever. Don't be mad at me about that guy. I was jealous, okay? I can be dirty too, if you want." Whoever said alcohol was a truth serum wasn't lying. He chuckles at my oversharing.

"We're here," he whispers, swinging open my door. He gently places me down on my bed.

"Lift your hands." I raise my arms and he pulls up my dress.

"Vincent, you really shaved your head." I put my hands on his head, rubbing the short scruff.

"Didn't I tell you I would?" His voice is low and deep as he gently pushes my hair back.

"But that was a while ago. I thought you forgot."

"I'll keep it shaved until we can be together openly. What do you think?"

I hiccup. "J-Janelle knows, now. And she's so mad...."

He licks his lips. "Because she loves you. Maybe you should tell her the truth. I don't want to isolate you from your sister."

He holds the back of my hair, staring at each feature of my face. "Why did you wear so much makeup tonight? I hated it." My stomach sinks at his displeasure.

"You did?" I raise my eyes to his nervously.

"Yes. Don't do it again." His voice is warm, but also sharp.

"But, everyone said it looked good. And that's how all the girls look here. I'm trying to fit in better—"

"How many times do I have to remind you? You aren't other girls. You'll never be other girls. When I look at you, I don't want to see them. They're fake, Eve. They've lost their innocence. You are nothing like them. Never will be."

"But, I want to be. I know the type you're used to..." I pause, my chest aching with the thought.

"No," he sighs, using his thumb to wipe my tears. "Don't you understand that you are my only type?"

I nod my head. "Okay, Vincent. No more makeup. Maybe just a little?"

He rolls his eyes and I shift to get under the covers. Pulling the comforter up and over me, he tucks it into my sides. I want to feel his lips on mine. His tongue in my mouth. Instead, he asks, "Do you have Advil?"

"Under the bed," I croak. I hear my plastic drawers opening and closing, and then the sink turning on. Finally, I feel his warm breath by my ear. "Sleep."

"Will you stay?"

"Not long. Can't bump into anyone in the morning." He moves behind me, pulling my body into his chest. I slide my legs between his so that we're entwined and let out a loud exhale. Vincent is my home.

"I wish you brought me to SoHo," I say quietly, nestling deeper into his chest.

"Me too. I was angry and wasn't thinking. Tomorrow night."

I hum my assent.

When I wake up, I turn to my bedside clock and see that it's five am. I sit up for a moment, my head pounding and muddled. I see the pills and a huge cup of water and immediately swallow them down. I'm not sure what was real and what was a dream last night. But when I put my nose into my pillow inhaling, I know Vincent was here.

CHAPTER 18

EVE

Vincent and I spend most of spring break in bed. I've cooked us every meal, and all we did was lounge around, make love, watch movies, and eat. We dance together too, because Vincent he knows how much I love it. He's tried a few times to discuss what happened at the club, but I told him I didn't want to talk about it. There's no use in rehashing Daniela's words when they do nothing but make me insecure.

Yesterday, I saw an episode on the *Food Network* of Giada making spaghetti Bolognese, and I wanted to make it for Vincent. I think he is going to be in heaven. At least, I hope so. I slice up a fresh baguette with garlic and olive oil, and pop it into the oven to get nice and crispy. The salad is already washed and sitting in the fridge.

I check the clock. Vincent will be home from his workout in about thirty minutes. While the sauce simmers, I decide now is a good time to wash up and get the smell of fried onions out of my hair.

I shower and then open up his side table to pull out a white T-shirt. It's snug on Vincent, but gigantic on me. I slide it on and grin; he loves when I wear his clothes, and I love it too. Just as I'm drying my hair with the towel, I hear the front door open and shut. "Hi honey, I'm home!" Vincent yells.

I laugh as he comes up behind me, but then cry out when I realize his shirt is soaked in sweat. "Ugh, Vincent! I just got clean, and now you're getting me all gross!" I'm trying to sound mad, but we both know I couldn't care less. I'll take him any way I can get him.

"Let me get you nice and dirty. I want you back in the shower with me."

"No. Dinner will be ready soon and I know you must be hungry."

"You know I love when you feed me. And the house smells fucking fantastic. But right now, I'm hungry for something else." He nips at my ear and my head rolls back.

An hour later, I'm drying my hair for the second time. I run into the kitchen to get everything ready for us while he makes some calls. Finally, he joins me by the stove, wearing jersey shorts and a T-shirt. His hair is still buzzed, making him look dangerous.

He moves to a seat and I bring everything to the table. "Goddamn, I'm a lucky man."

I smile and sit next to him. Vincent bows his head to say grace. I've never been religious before, but I know he grew up Catholic, and it's important to him. I press his cross against my chest, my own little version of a prayer.

We get to eating, and he groans that it's the best meal he's ever eaten.

"You really are an incredible cook. If law school doesn't work, there's always culinary school, huh?" I preen at his compliment. Looking down at his empty bowl gives me more satisfaction than I thought possible. If I could, I'd feed this man every single meal for the rest of my life. I know this is a negative for womankind and all, but cooking for him fulfills some emptiness inside my heart I didn't even realize existed. And watching him enjoy the food I made? Euphoria.

He pushes his chair closer to mine and I'm immediately assaulted by his amazing scent—fresh laundry and something purely Vincent.

He puts his hands in my hair, moving his fingers down to massage my neck. "Move in with me."

"I can't do that—"

"Why?" He wraps his hands around my face, smiling. He's genuine and delicious warmth. "Stay here. Bring your things over. You don't have to go back just because break is almost over."

He lets go of me and I crawl into his lap, nuzzling in his chest.

"I never want you anywhere else. In a few months, I'll be gone. I want to maximize our time together."

"But isn't it dangerous? Like, what if Daniela—"

"She won't know. She doesn't even know this apartment exists. And technically, you'll still have your room in the quad. I just don't wanna ask you to come over. I need to get home every night and have you here. In our home. I wanna wake up in the morning to you by my side. Drink my coffee with you."

"But the girls on my floor will start to wonder—"

"No, they won't. Didn't you tell me they're all in the middle of pledging sororities? Everyone makes all these friends first semester, but once they pledge, anyone who isn't in their sorority becomes a distant friend. That's the way it works here."

A smile spreads across my face and he laughs, his dark eyes twinkling. "I fucking love you. Want you in my bed every night of my life."

I curl myself around him. "It's gonna suck to be far from each other in a few months."

"Have you heard from any schools yet?" His voice is encouraging.

"Just waiting for interview dates. But you know, I can still apply to some places in Nevada—"

"No fuckin' way," he replies gruffly, dropping his fork. "We've discussed this already. I'm not letting you lower your standards, and California is close enough to where I'll be. You've worked all your life to get the best education; I'm not gonna be the reason you lose that."

His phone chimes, interrupting our conversation. He reads the message and curses. "Baby, I gotta go."

"No," I complain.

"Yes." He stands up with his plate in hand. "Dinner was amazing. Beyond fucking good. Don't throw out any of it. I want leftovers tomorrow or later tonight."

"I'm glad you liked it." I fuss with my hair as he proceeds to move everything from the table into the kitchen. "So, where are you going?" I know he never tells me, but…

"We've been through this." His hard voice shakes me back to reality. "Don't ask. When it's family business, it isn't yours." His voice is firm, with no room for negotiation.

My stomach clenches. I hate when he acts this way. Doesn't he understand I'm afraid he'll get hurt? What if the cops show up? Who would even be able to tell me if something went wrong?

He cleans the table silently, and I know he's gearing up for whatever is to come tonight. When he's done, he moves to the bedroom. I follow him into his walk-in closet, which I now know houses his weapons arsenal. Opening his gun safe, he methodically takes out holsters and guns. He takes off his clothes after dropping everything onto the bed. He's so strong and powerful, but I yearn to take care of him.

He moves to strap himself when I step in front of him. "Let me," I tell him softly. He blinks as I take his ankle holsters and drop to my knees, wrapping them above his feet. "Is this good?" I tighten them, staring up at him and biting my bottom lip.

He nods, handing me two small handguns that I slide inside and then fasten. Walking to his drawers, he pulls out a fresh black T-shirt and a pair of black jeans: his standard outfit when he leaves for business. He puts on another holster over his shirt, and I stand on my tippy-toes to tighten it for him. The straps make his muscles stand out even more than they normally do. I take two other guns off the bed and drop one in the left pocket and the other in the right. When the guns are secure, he pulls my hair back with his hands, forcing me to look into his eyes. I can only imagine what my face must be saying, because my heart is pounding and my core is pulsing. I want him so badly; I'm practically shaking.

As if a cloud passes through him, his eyes turn impossibly cold. I feel his breath against my lips, so imposing that I pause. I wouldn't dare move when he's in this zone.

He presses his lips to my ear. "Check the desk in the bedroom. I left something for you." His voice is curt, but I manage to nod my head. Stepping away from me, he takes a dark zip-up sweatshirt from his cabinet before striding out of the apartment. My stomach tenses as the door slams; he's gone.

Seemingly out of nowhere, I feel a pang for my sister. Vincent mentioned I should come clean and tell her everything. Now that he's not home, it's probably a good time. I pick up the phone to call her, biting my bottom lip nervously.

She answers after the first ring. "It's been almost three fucking weeks since your finals. I know you have no classes right now. So where have you been? I keep calling you and all I get in reply are some stupid texts telling me you're *okay*?" She's fuming. "You owe me a goddamn explanation!"

I fill her in on all the details. We cry together through the honest talk, but after over an hour of back and forth, she understands I'm going to take the risk for Vincent—no matter what. He and I are in this together, for the long haul. We're in love, and there's really nothing anyone can do or say at this point that can change that. Once she realizes that arguing with me is virtually impossible, she promises to try and get over it. Still though, she's angry at the choices I've made. I hang up, feeling relieved that at least Janelle finally knows. The lying was like a deadweight on my ankle.

Next, I call Claire, checking in to see how her break is going. She tells me she's unpacking and we make a plan for lunch between classes tomorrow. Even though I adore her, I don't think it's possible to maintain a true friendship when I hold secrets as big as the one I'm keeping. One of the things that saddens me the most about my situation with Vincent is because it's under the radar; we can't just live like a regular couple. I wished for a typical college life with studying and some parties, too, but I guess it isn't in the cards for me.

After cleaning up the dishes and saving the leftovers, I shuffle back into the bedroom to find a beautiful set of fresh keys with charms on a keychain, a list of security codes, and a note from Vincent.

Eve,

Keys to our apartment.

Everything that's mine is yours. Forever.

CHAPTER 19

VINCENT

I get into the car and force myself to change faces. It's whiplash moving between loving the hell out of my girl and having to take care of business. Tom keeps telling me something feels off at the ports, and his text said as much. In the business we're in, trusting our gut is necessary.

Daniela has been asking some probing questions ever since the club. Thank fuck Eve got herself off social media; if she saw what I've been doing these days, she'd probably go insane. Since Eve and Daniela had words, I've had to go the extra mile to keep Daniela off our backs. That means more time with her out in public, where I've been doing my best to keep her happy; at this point, I deserve a goddamn Oscar. Just tonight, I let her come with me to the gym, where she snapped a sweaty picture of the two of us after working out. She keeps insisting that Eve and I have something going on between us, but I just continue to deny it. The damage she can inflict is endless. Not fucking her definitely makes her angrier. I know she wants to get back with me—but that's not something I'll ever budge on.

I get to the stretch between Newark Liberty International Airport and Port Newark. The newspapers have described this area as the most dangerous two miles in America. They wouldn't be wrong. I open the car door and see Tom waiting for me, a smile on his hard face. I crack my neck side to side.

"Hey, brother." We knock our fists together. "I've got the rat. Motherfucker has been compiling some data for the Feds."

"Let's see him. Is he ready for me?"

He nods in the affirmative. I crack my knuckles.

CHAPTER 20

EVE

Spring break is now over. We only have eight weeks before the semester is finished, and then Vincent leaves for Nevada, and hopefully, I'll have transferred to a school out in California. Stanford is my top pick. I know some people would scoff at the idea of transferring schools for a man, but I don't see it that way. Vincent is my life, and if I can have both a great education and be closer to him, why shouldn't I try to do that?

I pour myself a hot cup of coffee from the dining hall, trying to stay calm—despite the fact I'm scared to death to bump into Daniela. The gossip mill says she went away with Chi Omega girls to Mexico. But now that she's back in the city, I'm not sure what to expect— especially after the club fiasco. Did she see Vincent run out of the club after me? Claire's warnings about her ability to ruin my life pound in my chest. Taking my coffee to go, I try to relax while walking to my first class of the day.

I take a seat in the center of the large lecture hall, pulling out my spiral notebook and a blue pen from my backpack. Strangely, a few students turn toward me before whispering to each other conspiratorially. I hope that it's my imagination, but I open up the mirror app on my phone anyway. Doing a quick scan of my teeth and face, I see nothing is out of the ordinary.

When class is over and I head out into the hallway, I bump into her. My gaze starts at her high-heeled black boots that tie up to mid-thigh, a short black skirt, and a beautiful cream-colored cashmere sweater; the color is bright against her perfectly tousled red hair. It hurts to admit it, but she looks like a million bucks.

My heart thuds as she looks down at me mockingly. "You poor thing." Daniela shrugs a bony and tanned shoulder. "You were totally wasted at the club before break. And the fact that it was photographed..."

"Photographed?"

"Well, you were dancing like a stripper. Do you even remember?" Her eyes move from my feet to my face disapprovingly. And then she lets out a little laugh as if I'm nothing but a joke.

"I—"

"Well, even if you don't, you should check *High and Low*. You're all over it. And let's just say, it isn't exactly flattering." She lifts a perfectly manicured hand up to her lips. "But then again, I guess you are who you are, right? I just hope the school doesn't find out about your behavior. I know they take scholarships away from kids like you who try to party with the rest of us."

Sweat breaks out on my forehead, but she continues, "It would be a shame if you got thrown out, wouldn't it? And after how hard you worked to get out of the ghetto you were raised in! What would your sister Janelle think if everything she sacrificed for you was all lost? Would you have to move back into the Blue Houses with your mom? She's a stripper too, right?"

My mouth drops open. How does she know? Cold terror moves straight down my spine and into my feet. Seemingly content with my obvious fear, Daniela struts off. I want to move, but I can't. I can barely breathe.

With a shaking hand, I manage to take out my phone and open the browser. I hear whispers in the hall, but I'm too focused on my task to pay attention. I quickly type in HIGH AND LOW in my Google search. I know this is what Daniela hoped for, but I need to know. I can't even think about anything other than finding out what is on the internet about me.

I click on the link, and there I am. Pages of photographs of me, dancing. My super-tight red dress leaves almost nothing to the imagination. A random guy stands flush behind me, his face slightly blurry. Every feature of mine is perfectly visible, though. As if the photos weren't enough, there's an article accompanying it.

Will Bitches Never Learn?

This freshman, Eve Petrov, was spotted before spring break at the hottest club in the city, Marquis. Word on the street is she tried to hook up with THE Vincent Borignone, who completely ignored her pathetic advances—obviously.

Bystanders at the club all laughed while she pounded shots, got completely wasted, and then slutted herself up to any guy who would give her attention. Ugh, gross!

When will this freshman girl learn more than just math? It's called self-respect. And by the way, no one told us here at High and Low that the drinking age was lowered to nineteen.

XOXO,

High and Low

I lift my head while mortification filters through my senses. I quickly type out a text to Claire. She responds right away, telling me to meet her by the no-smoking sign in front of Grant Hall—right now.

I run out of the building, not caring that people are watching. I burst through the front doors of the mathematics building, wanting to collapse in relief when I see Claire waiting by the tree.

She starts, "I read it. Everyone has. So, swallow your pride and let's figure out how to deal now, okay?" I nod my head. We're in crisis mode, but she's in control. It almost feels as if I'm an outsider looking in. My mind hasn't caught up to the fact that this is all happening to me.

"First thing you do, is a lot of really good stuff so when your name comes up in a Google search, the newer and more positive stuff about you comes up first. That means getting your name out wherever possible in conjunction with good things. Like, charities. Or, donating your time to a good cause. We don't ever want a future employer seeing this!"

The tears well up in my eyes. "Employer?" I gasp. This is my future. My life! What if one of the schools I plan on transferring to sees this?

She puts a hand on my shoulder. "It is what it is, Eve. Another thing you need to do is to speak to Vincent. Maybe he can find a way to erase it."

"B-but how?" I stutter.

"People have connections. I have no idea who is behind *High and Low*, but you never know. Girls would lick the dirty gym floor if Vincent asked them to do it. If he knows who wrote it, I bet they'd take it down if he asked. It's worth a try. At least your friendship can help you in this way, right?" She looks at me accusingly, but I drop down on the grass, bringing my knees to my chest.

She sighs, sitting down next to me. "Text him now, Eve." I look up to see urgency in her face. I can tell she knows I've been lying, but she has the decency not to mention it right now.

Pulling out my phone, I text Vincent, asking him to call me when he can. Three minutes later, my phone rings.

"Eve?" His voice is soft and warm, how it gets in the morning right when he wakes.

I start before I lose the nerve. "I'm on *High and Low*. Can you find a way to get it taken off?" My voice comes out in a rush. I'm not just mortified. I'm also ashamed.

"They wrote about you?" He sounds furious.

"That gossip site. They said…" I pause. I want to tell him everything, but I'm too upset to speak. I swallow the dryness in my mouth, willing myself to hold it all in until I get to the privacy of my dorm room.

"Give me a few hours. It'll be gone." He hangs up the phone. I'm sitting on the ground with Claire by my side. She takes my hand.

"Vincent to the rescue, huh?" Her smile is relieved, but also sad.

"Do you really think he'll get it removed?" My desperation is making my head pound, the tears finally starting to fall.

"Yes. I do." She's nodding, the hopefulness written all over her face. "But Eve, please stay away from him. If Daniela is out to get you, this is likely just the tip of the iceberg. Getting her angry is a really bad thing. She's so connected, Eve. I tried to warn you, and I hope it's not too late."

"I'm gonna go back to my room. I can't be out on campus right now."

I run-walk directly to the quad with my head down, swiping my key card to get into the building. After climbing the steps, I bump into my Resident Advisor. She's about to say something, but I quickly run past her; I can barely look up. Has she seen it? Has everyone?

I sit at the desk in my room, opening my computer and checking out *High and Low*. Tears of relief fall down my face when I see that the article and all the photos about me are gone.

CHAPTER 21

VINCENT

Slamming my hand on my desk, I pace the length of my bedroom. I'm back in my apartment by school, here to grab a textbook for Number Theory. The fact that Eve was on *High and Low*—and her name was mentioned in connection with mine—is a huge goddamn problem. Thankfully, I know the girls who run it. The moment I told them to remove the photos and the article, they took it all down. But if Daniela saw the article, there will be hell to pay.

My doorbell rings, and I open the door to see her. The bitch has timing; I'll give her that. I take a deep breath as she waltzes into my apartment.

"Vincent." She drops her designer purse on the floor carelessly.

"Daniela."

Sitting on the edge of the couch, she crosses her legs—high-heeled boots and a skirt so short it's practically indecent.

"I saw you got that article taken down. So, contrary to everything you've told me, you obviously care about her."

"Care? She's no one to me," I scoff. "Now do me a favor and get out. I've got work to do."

"You think you can just get rid of me? You're funny, Vincent. Do you know how many men would give their right arm to get me in bed?" She puts her arms on her hips.

"Good for you, then." I laugh angrily. "Go fuck whoever you want." I walk into my kitchen, pulling out a bottle of water from the fridge.

She trails behind me. "Look at me," she says, grabbing my arm. "Me and you go together. Me and you are together. We. Are. Together."

I shake my head slowly, amazed that a girl this smart in the books can be so delusional. "We aren't anything, Daniela. Not now and not ever. You need to find another man and move on. I'm sick of this bullshit." I can feel the tendons straining in my neck. I know I need to calm down, but it's becoming damn near impossible.

"Another man? What other man? Look in the mirror, Vincent! Me and you make sense. Me and you are perfect. Our families—think about the connections! We'd rule the world. I totally accept your life. Hell, I more than accept it. I love it. We," she starts, gesturing between us, "make sense!" Her lashes flutter faster than normal; the girl is unhinged and clearly on something.

I put the bottle to my lips, swallowing the entire thing down.

"It's her! That fucking bitch charity case!" She's panting. "You think I'm blind? I saw how you looked at her at the club before break, Vincent. I know you bought her that fucking jacket! You help her with her studying. I already knew you were fucking her, but I figured she was a passing fling!"

"You need to be committed to a mental hospital, Daniela. She and I have nothing between us." The lie burns my throat.

She starts moving through my room, emptying drawers. "Does she have her shit in your room? Is she here every night in your bed, where I'm supposed to be?" She runs into my bedroom like a dog on a scent, throwing my drawers open and pulling out my clothes.

"Calm the fuck down!" I yell. My shirts and underwear are scattered around the room.

"Calm down?" she seethes, facing me with her fists balled up at the sides. "Don't tell me to fucking *calm* down! You swore to me you'd never bring another girl into our orbit. You could fuck anyone you wanted, so long as it didn't infringe on what we have. And when I get calls from my friends telling me that my man is staring at another girl and I better get my ass to the club to intercept it? People are going to think there is trouble between us! People are going to think we're breaking up! I saw how you looked at her. I watched you go after her in that club after she was dancing with that guy!" Tears start to fall down her face.

"Jesus FUCK Daniela. You don't own me! I'm done with you. Get out!"

She stands tall, a smirk growing on her lips. "First, I'm going to call my father to pull the plug on your business. Second? I'm going to get that whore of yours thrown out of school for indecent behavior. I read up on the expectations of scholarship kids. Underage drinking? That's *academic probation*. And third? I'm going to publicly humiliate her. I will make sure the entire world knows that she. Is. A. Homewrecker!" Her breaths turn shallow and hard. "You think you can walk away from me? Humiliate me with some piece-of-shit loser?"

I step up to her. "Have you forgotten who I am?" My voice is terrifyingly low; I feel my jaw clench. My anger is catching hold of me. Part of my brain is telling me to calm the fuck down, but the other side is only getting hotter until my judgment is officially clouded over.

"A-are you threatening me?" Her voice turns shrill.

I pull out my gun from the waistband of my jeans. Pushing her against the wall, muzzle pressed underneath her neck. "Who the fuck do you think you are, Daniela? If you so much as even *attempt* to do what you just said, I will end your fucking life." She shudders, but I don't let up. "What? You think I'm going to be shitting in my pants over some dumb bitch like you? You think you can control me?"

I step back and she falls forward, tripping over her own feet and landing on the floor. Hysterical, she grabs her purse and runs out of my room, the front door slamming against the wall with a *bang*. I laugh as she runs.

***

I've been stewing for hours, pacing my room and going through every possible scenario that could go wrong when I get a call from Tom on my work phone.

"Yo."

"Serious trouble here at the port, man."

"What are you talking about?" My breath turns shallow. "Didn't we already deal with the rat?"

"Yeah, but someone is stalling our shipment out of Columbia. We were ready to accept today, but the flight turned around mid-fucking-air. My dad told me to call Antonio right away to let him know, but I wanted to let you know first. This isn't because of Daniela, right Vincent? Because I think one of the Feds infiltrated a labor union here, too. I can feel shit going down—"

"Got it. Thanks." I hang up the phone, cursing.

I pick my work phone back up, dialing my driver. I have to see my father. I check the time and know he must be home right now. I throw on a sweatshirt and take the stairs to my building's lobby; I've got a shit ton of energy right now I need to expend.

The car ride to the townhouse is quick. I grew up here, on Ninety-Third Street between Madison and Fifth Avenue. Unlocking the front doors, I strut through the hallways lined with money. Famous art hangs to my left and right, each piece valued between thirty-thousand to close to a million.

I stop in the living room and take a seat on a navy velvet couch, a red and blue Persian rug under my feet. My father will call me when he's ready; he knows I'm here. In fact, I'd bet he's watching me on the security camera right now. I breathe deeply, getting my head on straight.

"Vincent," my father's stern voice calls out on speakerphone. "Come down."

I exhale as I get to the staircase, walking down two flights of carpeted stairs into the basement level. Opening the second door to the left, I enter our meeting room. The walls are painted in black lacquer and a huge crystal chandelier hangs from the center, giving the room a dark glow. He sits in his black leather chair at the head of the table. In this moment, he's no one other than the leader and boss of the Borignone mafia, and I can tell from his body language he's angry as all fuck.

"I'm waiting for an explanation as to how all of this shit broke down. I already heard from some of our friends that Costa was behind stalling our shipment today. You're my right hand. Who the fuck is causing a crack in the empire I've built? Tell me you didn't piss off the daughter, Vincent." Sitting tall in one of his custom suits, he stares at me with fury in his eyes. He brings his cigarette to his lips, taking a heavy drag. The smoke wafts through his lips and nose, momentarily covering his face. I can tell he knows. He's waiting for the confirmation.

Without any preamble, I begin with the night Eve and I met. I fill him in on the important details, including what happened to her at the hands of Carlos and the fact that we're together right now, in secret. I end with Daniela's threats.

His breaths turn shallow as he drops his head, seemingly gathering himself. "Do you know what you've just done?" His voice is low, eyes turning to thin slashes in his face. "And for a piece of pussy? I expected more from you, Vincent. You aren't one of these dumb fucking kids who can't think without his dick!" He slams his fists against the table. "I raised you better than that! We had a vote. You weren't supposed to fuck shit up with her!"

"I'm a man. Not Daniela's bitch!" I spit out. "She doesn't control us, and she sure as fuck doesn't control me," I yell back.

"Ah, so now my son is twenty-two and knows it fuckin' all, huh? Our entire business is shaking right now because of this bitch! I don't need to remind you we've got three hundred kilos of cocaine on that plane. That's close to fifteen million dollars." His red face flashes.

"And on top of that, Lieutenant Wall called. The Feds are gathering evidence to file a suit against us under RICO. They're trying to bar us from any business involvement at the ports and in any union activity around the harbors. They're catching on about the unions being in our back pockets; according to all the shit Enzo has picked up, they're not going to grab us on drug trafficking, but instead, embezzlement of union funds."

I look up at his angry face. "For RICO, they'll need to show a pattern of racketeering activity. Do you think they've put surveillance inside the unions?" I pause, my mind running as it puts together different possibilities. If they've been listening in on union activity, we're completely fucked. We are so closely tied to labor that they're essentially another arm of our organization.

He grips the side of the table. "They don't need to prove criminal acts. All they need is to focus on behavioral patterns. Patterns, Vincent. That isn't difficult to show. And now that you've fucked with Costa's daughter, we've got another fight on our hands." The cords in his neck strain. "If we don't get him to send our flights back here, we'll be taking a huge hit."

I swallow hard, my mouth completely dry. "The RICO case is just a continuing vendetta by the government to try to throw our name around. There have been decades of investigations, which have led nowhere. Maybe they're just trying to scare us—"

"The threat is real. And I'm going to bet that within the week they'll take in the labor officials. The FBI is knocking on our goddamn door. We've had a chokehold on shipping and all other waterfront activities for the last sixteen fuckin' years, and we're gonna to have to give them something."

"If they bar us from activity in the ports, they'd basically be putting an entire marketplace under court supervision. That's just not possible. All businesses will stall." Sweat beads on my forehead, dripping down the sides of my face.

"It's possible. And it's happening."

I drop my head into my hands. Everything I prayed wouldn't happen, just did.

"And Costa controls half of South America. Look what he was able to do within moments of you fighting with his daughter! Turning our planes around? Fuck!" He slams his hand back down on the table. "He's obviously waiting for our phone call to clear up this goddamn mess!"

I exhale, trying to stay focused. "Call him. He'll want a bigger cut of the money we give him to launder and house. That should be enough to shut him up and free up our shipment." I grind my teeth, internally agonizing.

He stands before grabbing the phone; I can see a tremor in his hand. *Millions of dollars could be lost because of me.*

He tells Costa not to let the squabble of kids fuck up the goodwill they've got going on between them. I can hear Costa yelling through the phone. They go back and forth until finally agreeing that Costa will keep thirty-five percent of all monies sent to him for laundering. He'll also release the plane within the hour. My father hangs up the phone, pulling out his gun and aiming it straight to my head.

"You realize the loss we're taking? You fucked up big time, Vincent." He says my name like a curse; if I weren't his son, he would shoot me in the head. He brings the gun back down and lights up another cigarette.

***

An hour later, twelve of us sit together around the table. Smoke billows around the room as my father updates the family. Everyone talks over each other, enraged that I went against their orders and pissed off Daniela. I'm not sure they realize that Costa is essentially turning into the largest shareholder of Borignone mafia. Now that he's taking this much of our profits, we all have to wonder who works for whom. Luckily, my father doesn't mention Eve in connection with all this drama. If anyone knew she was the reason all of this went down, it wouldn't bode well for her.

My father clears his throat. Voices simmer, but the anger level is still high. "It's fucking horrible what's happened, but it's done. We gotta send Vincent out to Nevada as soon as possible to start gaming and get us out of Costa's hold. We also gotta discuss this potential RICO charge that Enzo believes is coming on the quick."

Hell is pouring down. My shirt is soaked in sweat, but I continue to keep myself looking controlled. I can't let my emotions rule me.

Enzo shifts in his seat. He has the same sandy-blonde hair and big build as Tom, but probably fifty pounds heavier. "At least one of us has to go to lockup, Antonio. Someone needs to plead guilty to a lesser charge, or we risk seizure of all our assets under RICO. And I'm not talking about soldiers we can pay off to do time. The Feds are going to want someone from around this table." My father turns to me pointedly, a cigarette dangling from the corner of his mouth. I can tell what he's thinking. Tom warned me. Hell, I knew the consequences when I got into it with Eve, but I took the risk anyway. My day of reckoning has come. I may not have been the one to tip off the Feds about our union involvement, but the fact that my fuck-up led to giving Costa this much of our money is all my doing.

"I'll do it." My voice comes out clear.

They all shift in their seats and stare at me, faces hard as stone. "I'll go," I repeat.

"No," my Enzo declares firmly. "The build-out in Nevada is the most important thing on our agenda. And you're the only one with the key because of your birthright. If you're in lockup, we'll be stuck with Costa for another goddamn decade."

"I'll still be able to work; I don't need to physically live out west to get it done. If I hire a lawyer to do business on my behalf, through a power of attorney, I can do it all from prison. I'm sure we can even arrange weekly meetings, too. Nothing about what I'm doing out west is illegal on its face; in fact, by design, it's one hundred percent kosher. We can all rest assured that within five to seven years, the complex will be operating and we can be free of that fuck."

Luciano's voice clears from the end of the table. "What if you get hurt? If somethin' happens to you in lockup, there will be no casino complex."

Everyone starts talking again, turning to each other in debate.

I clear my throat loudly. "Let's put it to the table. Let's vote." My voice is strangely calm.

"Why don't we send Tommy in there with him?" Luciano chimes in.

Enzo shrugs. "Not a bad thought. My son won't leave Vincent's side. Plus, we've got seven soldiers already in Canaan. We'll cut a deal to make sure the boys go there so they'll have protection."

"There's something else," Luciano says. "In Canaan, they've got tough regulations for e-mail and internet access. If we send Vincent, they've got to lax those rules for him. Otherwise, he won't be able to work."

"True," Enzo replies. "Let's make sure to bring that up with Goldsmith when he works out the plea deal. That's gotta be non-negotiable. In writing."

"And how about Daniela?"

Luciano shifts in his chair. "She'll find a way to spin it in her favor. Of that, I have no fuckin' doubt. Anyway, shit with her is done, right? Antonio worked out that deal with Costa; his daughter's feelings don't matter to us no more." The men nod and grumble in agreement.

A part of my chest loosens. The days of Daniela owning me are done.

My father leans back in his chair and lets out a deep breath. "A'right. I'm gonna call Goldsmith. Let's get everything organized with him quickly. I'd say Vincent and Tom have about a week. Vincent, you think that's enough time to get your shit in order?"

Enzo chuckles. "It's gotta be enough. Right now, RICO is a hard threat. We gotta stop that train before it runs us over."

I crack my knuckles, one by one. The men all stand to leave, shaking my father's hand and then mine, as they exit the room. I'm taking the fall, which means I'll have paid my debt for this fuck-up.

Once the men are gone, my father sits up. "Prison." He shakes his head as if in shock and picks up another cigarette.

I pull his pack toward me, taking out a smoke for myself and light up. I take a deep inhale, thinking about the fact that I'll be behind bars for God knows how many years of my life. My exhale is long and slow. *What have I just signed up for?*

"We've all been there. And you're tough. Sergey will make sure to give you pointers before entering; he'll show you how to make weapons, too. Once you've established yourself, general pop will leave you alone. They will know who you are, and you'll have proven your worth. After that, it's just time. Time where you can get everything moving for Gaming. Whatever you need done from the outside, we'll make sure it goes through."

I nod my head, keeping my gaze strictly on him, and letting him know with my eyes that I'm both hearing and listening to his words.

He leans back in his seat. "I met her, you know. She was at Angelo's. I scared the shit outta her. Let me tell you, that girl looked at me like I was the fuckin' devil," he chuckles.

I look at him questioningly, wondering what he's getting at.

"Going to jail makes many alliances, but also many enemies. And a girl like her?" He raises his eyebrows. "I don't have to tell you that plenty of men would want to take her. Especially to retaliate."

Blood rushes into my head and my stomach churns. I clench and then unclench my fists. He has his own reasons for wanting her out of my life. Of that, I'm sure. Still though, he has a real point. I shuffle in my seat, not wanting him to see that my chest is caving in. If anyone knew I had a woman I was leaving behind…if she even came to prison for a visit…it could mean her death.

He puts his hand out to me, and I steel myself, shaking it firmly. Before I can let go of his grip, he squeezes my palm. "Get shit set for Gaming so you won't lose any time while you're locked up. The sooner we get it off the ground, the sooner we can cut Costa loose."

He's all business. I nod my head, swallowing hard. "I'll send you hard copies of my plans, and I'll scan and email myself everything. I already discussed with Erez about how many men we'll need to pressure the Tribal Council. As we discussed, it'll probably be bloody getting them to agree to this."

"You going away is a fucking travesty for the entire family, Vincent. You'll come out stronger, though. No room in this life for love. Love is for pussies. Prison will teach you." He holds my hand for another beat and then releases me.

I move to leave, when he clears his throat. "One more thing. Tomorrow morning, you gotta get inked. It's time to get the Borignone insignia."

"I'll call Shane, then."

He looks at me gravely. With a swift nod to the leader of the Borignone mafia, I walk out the door, my fate sealed.

CHAPTER 22

VINCENT

I take a car to the East River at Eighty-Seventh Street, sit back on a bench, and light up a smoke while staring at the lights of the RFK Bridge.

Eve accepted me and my life months ago. She won't be easily convinced to be done with me; even if I'm in jail, she'll want to stay close. And she'd wait the however many years if I asked her to wait. I know this because I'd wait a lifetime for her.

I have to break her heart—make sure she believes we're completely done. I need her to get off the East Coast, and then promptly forget I ever existed. If she has any hope, she'll hang onto me. If there's one thing my father is right about, it's this: if anyone hears there is a woman I love, they will come for her and use her against me. Not least, I wouldn't be able to sleep knowing she's waiting—for potentially ten goddamn years—for me to leave prison. What if I die in lockup? What if I come out a different man completely? She can't wait. I won't let her.

My father's reasons for that good advice are obviously purely selfish. He sees her as the girl who shook our empire. I lift my head for a moment, realizing that the biggest threat of all may be him—Antonio Borignone. She has to leave and my father must know that it's completely over. It's shocking to imagine that my father would do that to me. But when he puts on that suit, he's only one man—the Boss. And the Boss makes sure every *I* is dotted and every *T* is crossed.

I exhale, wondering how I'm going to break us up. I imagine that the plan is for a fictional character, because every time I think of doing this to my girl, my stomach clenches.

Finally, I pick up the phone, calling Angelo. I'm going to need him to back up my story. I know how close they are, and he's the best man for the job as she trusts him entirely.

He listens intently to me before cursing me out. The only reason why I accept the way he's speaking is because I know it's out of love for my girl. He's furious I dragged her into this mess in the first place. He's shocked, but his fury only solidifies the truth; Eve deserves better than me and this life. When the conversation ends, I hang up the phone and drop my head into my palms.

All of a sudden, I'm assaulted by the memory of Eve's shitty stairwell back in the Blue Houses. I haven't thought of that shithole in quite some time. My breath grows ragged, imagining those darkened steps.

***

I move behind her, one hand on my piece and the other at her lower back. I feel her tiny frame trembling at my touch. I want to turn her around and pull her into my arms, grab her and carry her up to her apartment. No, I want to grab her and carry her out of this fuckin' shithole. I just need to feel her lips on mine. Everything about her calls to me. She's whip-smart and intellectual and somehow, has no goddamn clue how gorgeous she is. My heart pounds with want. She's so tiny, and it brings out the caveman in me. Even two steps behind her, I tower over her.

I turn her around on the step and do my best to gauge her mood in the dark. Could I leave her in this building alone tonight? What I see in her face has my dick twitching; she wants me. Full lips parted, eyes slightly glazed. I go in for a soft kiss, not wanting to scare her. But the minute we touch, it's as if I've been electrocuted. Never in my life have I felt heat and energy like this.

***

My mind flashes to Eve in my kitchen, cooking for us a few nights ago.

"Vincent!" *she squeals, running and jumping into my arms as though she hasn't seen me in a year. We were just together this morning. I laugh at her exuberance.* "I'm making you the best dinner. Wash up and sit!"

I drop my backpack on the floor by the table and then move to the sink to wash my hands.

Turning, I watch as Eve pulls a foil-covered dish out of the oven using a set of black oven mitts that I never even knew I owned.

She's so beautiful. Fuck. I stand up and move behind her as she places the dish on the counter. Using my fingers, I pull off a piece of chicken straight out of the pan, like I know she hates.

"Vincent, no!" *she scolds, trying to push me back.*

"Eve, yes!" *I mimic her voice, chuckling as I take another juicy bite.*

"Don't eat like an animal. Let me put it all out for us; I just need a few more minutes to take the rice off the stove."

"I'm a growing boy. I can't wait, and you're moving too slow."

"You have zero patience, has anyone ever told you that?"

"Nope." *I take another bite, trying not to laugh.*

"You're a liar."

"Wait, Eve. Shush. Do you hear that sound?" *I move my eyes left to right.*

"Hear what?" *She cocks her head to the side, listening intently.*

"It's my stomach growling. It's angry, Eve."

"Oh, Vincent. Sit your ass down."

"My ass or your ass?" I grab her, lifting her onto the counter.

"Let go! I need to take the rice off, or it'll burn."

"You're giving me your bitch face. You know I love that face." I nuzzle my nose into her neck, inhaling.

She pushes me back and I let her move me.

Lifting an arched eyebrow, she fumes in that sexy way of hers.

"Okay, okay, I'll sit." I bring her down from the counter and move to my seat, watching her fuss over my meal, staring as she mixes the salad. Watching as she scoops out the rice with a fork before tasting it, making sure it's just right. Mine.

***

I blink, feeling wetness coat my cheeks.

CHAPTER 23

VINCENT

I arrive to SoHo and see Eve curled in the fetal position over my covers; she's fast asleep. "Eve. Are you awake?" I drop to my knees by the bed and put my nose by her throat, breathing in her scent. I don't want to touch her when my clothes smell like smoke and sweat.

She opens her eyes, groggy from sleep. "Vincent? You're home. I was so worried about you."

"Eve, do you remember the buried art?" I'm remembering a few months back when we were studying together. I had to write a paper on lost art during World War II. I explained to Eve how people buried their valuables in their backyards before they were taken by the Nazis. They were hoping that one day, if they made it home, they could find their valuables again. I wish there was a way to bury what we had underground instead of burning it to ash. I'm selfishly praying that somehow, she retains just a sliver of hope. Just enough that if I happen to make it out of prison alive, we may have a chance again.

"Mm hmm," she says as she snuggles down, immediately falling back asleep.

I remove my clothes and take a hot shower before putting on a fresh pair of boxers. Before getting into bed, I rifle through her purse to find our apartment keys. Holding the keychain up to the light, I pull off one of the charms, a silver boot. This charm, above all others, has a deeper meaning for me. I want her to know that I'd follow her anywhere. And, I want it to keep her safe when she leaves here. Pulling it off the key ring, I drop the charm into the small zipper pocket inside her purse. I need to know that whatever happens to these keys, the charm will stay with her.

I get in bed, pulling her under the covers with me. Checking the time, I see it's after one in the morning.

I want to wake her. Make love to her. Moving some hair away from her face, I can see her eyelids flutter; she's back in a deep sleep. I move my lips to her ear. I know she can't hear me, but I need to tell her anyway.

"Eve," I exhale, burrowing my nose behind her ear. "I want to take you to be my wife." Kiss. "I want to have you and hold you." Kiss. "From this day forward, for better, for worse." Kiss. "For richer, for poorer, in sickness and in health." Kiss. "Until death do us part." Kiss. "I'm so sorry for what I'm about to do. Forgive me, baby. I love you so fucking much." I fall asleep with my face buried in her coconut-scented hair, wishing things could be different, but knowing that come morning, I'll be shattering her life, and mine.

I wake up to pots and pans banging in the kitchen. I stand up and stretch for a moment before brushing my teeth. Washing up quickly, I can feel the clock ticking between my ears. I need to do this right away before I lose my nerve. This is about saving her and giving her the best possible life.

"Hi." I lean against the kitchen counter, arms folded across my chest. She's fluttering around, opening and closing cabinets and flipping eggs like this place is her home.

She beams at me. "You're awake!"

Is this the last time I'll see her smile? I blink. "We have to talk. You're skipping classes today."

Her large brown eyes squint in question. "What's wrong? Is everything okay?" She pours an oversized mug full of black coffee and fills a plate with eggs. She tries to hand them to me, but I don't take them from her.

Gone is the Vincent with stars in his eyes. In a matter of one night, I've managed to drown my old self. Resurrected is the man who does nothing other than represent the toughest mafia in the country.

"Do you know who I am?"

"Of course I know who you are. But, you aren't just one thing—"

I cut her off. "That's where you're wrong. I'm always Vincent Borignone."

"I- I don't understand." Her gaze moves from my feet up to my eyes, finally taking in my hard demeanor. She steps back, dropping the plate and cup on the countertop. They clang against the marble and I clench my fists, trying to stay straight.

"The Feds are coming after us. And I'm going to be taken in. Less than a week. I'm meeting with my lawyer tomorrow and we'll probably meet with the FBI the day after."

"Taken in? B-but—"

"I'm going to prison, Eve. Between seven to ten. Shit went down with Daniela and me after *High and Low*, and she ran to her father. He stalled a huge shipment. It all happened in tandem with a huge investigation into the ports by the FBI." I clench my fists. "One of us needs to plead guilty to a lesser charge before they bring forward a RICO case, and I'm the one who is going to take the fall."

"N-no. No, Vincent. You can't. It's not possible." I can see her pulse flutter in her neck.

"I'll be gone, and who knows what Daniela may do to you. You need to finish this year with your head down and leave for California like you originally planned."

"I don't care about her. I'll pull my applications and stay here with you. I only wanted to transfer because you were going to Nevada—"

I huff, stopping her from continuing. "We're finished, Eve. You wanna stay here and let Daniela ruin your life? Be my guest. She knows all about you, now. And it's only a matter of time before she goes public about us."

"No." She vehemently shakes her head. Her ponytail loosens, stray hairs falling in front of her face. I want to brush it out of her eyes, but I won't. I can't. "Forget her. I don't care about her, Vincent!"

I let out a hostile breath. "Do you know what I did a few weeks ago?" I step closer to her, my body language angry. "I personally took a knife to Rafa Vasquez's throat. Slit him from here…to here." I graze my middle finger across her beautiful narrow neck. "Then threw him off a boat myself. He's a captain in the Cartel. You remember the Cartel, don't you, baby?

"They've been skimming some cocaine off our shipments. Their entire gang has a vendetta against me, now. And that's just the beginning. We've spoken of who I am. What I do. But maybe you don't remember, huh?" I keep my hands loose around her throat, but still tight enough that she knows who's in control. "When Daniela tells the world about you, who do you think is gonna come knocking on your door? *The Cartel*. And where will I be? Behind bars."

"No, Vincent," she whispers. "You're my life. I- I can't live without you. Don't push me away. I know that side of you exists, but soon we'll be gone together. I can wait here. If I go, I'll never be able to visit—"

I laugh sardonically. "You think I'm a good man. You don't know who I am. What I do. You conveniently ignore it." My breath is low as I methodically rub my thumb back and forth across her neck, wanting to both strangle her and love her. I hate her for what she's done to me. She makes me weak. She makes me fucking insane with love and lust. Instead of panicking, she shuts her eyes and raises her head, offering herself to me.

"Vincent," she whimpers. "I'm here. I'm right here."

I'm on her in seconds.

Tick-tock. Tick-tock. Time pounds at my ears.

It's messy. Teeth clanking. Desperate. Dropping on the wooden floor, I strip her completely naked, tearing her underwear off. I pull down my pants, sliding into her soft and willing body.

I spend the rest of the day inside her, but my anger won't stop pulsing through my veins. Nothing is lessening my need. I'm squeezing her too tightly. I'm holding her too roughly. I'm sucking on her perfect skin too hard. But I won't stop myself. I just can't. And she takes it all. Letting me do what I want. Giving me her essence. Offering herself up to me.

The reality of what will happen bangs against my chest—she must leave, forget me, not contact me again—but my body is refusing to listen. Not right now. Not fuckin' yet.

Tick-tock. Tick-tock.

"Moan for me how I like. I want to hear you." I drag her to the edge of the bed and drop down to the floor. I take a long, deep lick out of her center. I taste both of us on her, and it only spurs me on. I have to memorize this moment. Memorize *her*.

"Vincent," she pants. Her legs are shaking so hard I have to hold them down. I know how sensitive she is, but I need her to take everything I'm giving. *She tastes so fucking good.* Her chest rattles in pleasure and pain; she grips the sheets, trying to keep herself from crying out again as she thrashes her head from side to side. It's too much. Her voice, hoarse, echoes around the room.

I finally let her go, moving back up and drawing her small body into mine. Her dark hair sticks to the sweat on my chest, but I lock her down so she can't move a muscle without my consent.

"Oh, Vincent," she cries. "I'm here, baby. I'm here. I won't leave you. Never."

I come inside her so many times, I'm convinced I've found my way into her bloodstream. She's my salvation. *How am I going to walk away from her?* I try to fuse our naked bodies together with my strength, moving my head so she can't see my face. Would she be able to see my pain? I know how much larger I am than her, but nothing is enough.

I turn her onto her back. She's so fragile. Perfect. I let my hands roam all over her body and stop at her flat stomach. I bend down to lick and kiss her smooth skin. I span my fingers around her waist, wishing she were pregnant right now with my child. I want love and intimacy and home-cooked meals. I want all of it with Eve, every day forever.

Instead, I'm leaving for prison. Giving up a decade of my life. The only way to survive in there is to give up my humanity. While I'm in lockup, I can be nothing other than cold-blooded. I need to let myself adapt to the change. Having a woman like her in the back of my mind would only weaken me.

While I'm kissing her, I let myself imagine her here in the city while I'm behind bars. I picture my enemies finding out about her and then, coming after her. Or my father, taking her away to punish me. My heart pounds, solidifying my decision.

I have only one fear in this world, and it isn't dying or being tortured. It's that my love will haunt her. Have I put a mark on her head? I was supposed to leave her alone. I should never have insisted on us being together. I was impulsive and reckless.

She lays on top of me. Breathing hard. Hands roaming up and down my biceps.

"Vincent?"

I move my head to see her. Something that looks like hope fills her large brown eyes. She brings her hands to my shoulders, so gentle.

"Don't make me go. I can't leave you. Don't you understand?"

"I gotta do what needs to be done. You have to leave for California, and not look back." I want her to scream at me and tell me that we're done. I need to hear her say she wants nothing to do with a murderer. I want her to slap me across the face, angry I had sex with her so savagely, and run out of this apartment. "Please," my heart begs.

She shakes her head. "No. I'm not leaving you. I can't! It's just not possible!" She moves over me, straddling my legs. "Once you're out of prison, we'll live out on the reservation together, right? I want to live far from everything and everyone. I've dealt with far worse shit my whole life. I can handle this."

Her words feel like a sucker punch to the gut. The plan has to stay in play. She isn't going to give me up. I remove her hands from my chest and stand; I need to get away from her.

"Vincent?" She sits up in the bed, but I move quickly.

I open my drawers, turning away from her in both mind and body. Pulling out a fresh pair of jeans and a long-sleeve gray Henley, I slide it on as if the love of my life isn't breaking down in front of my eyes. Hurting her right now feels like I'm cutting off my own arm, but I ignore it. Overriding every emotion in my heart is my need to keep her safe.

I pause for a moment to breathe. I want to press my lips against the cross around her neck and swear to her and Jesus that I'll be back for her. That she belongs to me. That I'll never love anyone else other than her. But I can't.

I hear her heavy breaths while fat tears drop down her face. "Don't, Vincent. Don't do this to me. I know you love me. You can't pull this cold routine anymore. You need me to stay close to you." She gets out of bed, walking on my heels as I step into the bathroom to brush my teeth. I stare at our reflection in the mirror; I double her in size. "Tell me you love me, Vincent," she begs, hands up in prayer.

I stay silent. Squeeze toothpaste on the bristles. Brush. Turn on the faucet. Put my hands into the water like a cup and draw it into my mouth. Swish. Spit. Clean the brush.

I turn around and see she's on her knees in front of me, crying. She clutches my calves, head bent to my legs. "I want to wait for you. However long it takes—"

"No, Eve. We're done. We had a good time while it lasted, but you have to move on. I'm done with you now." I bend down, grabbing her shoulders. Doing a quick survey of her body, I can clearly see all the bruises that I've placed on her with my mouth and hands. What have I done? I deserve jail after what I'm about to put her through. I let go of her and she collapses to the floor.

I walk out the door, leaving her broken, no traces of mercy behind me. I have to pray that maybe one day, she'll forgive me.

***

I'm on the couch at my apartment by school. Picking up my phone, I call Tom. At least I have no doubts of his loyalty. My brother will be by my side until the end.

"Come over tonight to my SoHo loft. Bring girls. There's something I need to do." I scratch the back of my head with my free hand.

"Yeah, no shit. We've got a limited time to fuck as much as we can. Or at least, I do. And by the way, fuck you, Vincent! Fuck you for dragging us into this shit and fuck that bitch for fucking it all up!"

I can imagine Tom's hands shaking on the other end of the line. He may be angry, but he's tough as fuck and will do just fine with me in prison. "One way or another, we'd have to do time for the family. Every man has done it. Now it's our turn."

"Well, I didn't want to go now! How about that, motherfucker!"

"Don't spend your last few days of freedom complaining like a pussy. I'm heading over now to Shane's to get inked. Then meeting with Goldsmith to discuss what we're going to plead. Tonight though, let's party." With the thought of this evening, my teeth clench together; I can feel the vibration in the back of my skull.

"I'll be there," he growls.

I hang up and the rest of my afternoon runs in a blur. By ten o'clock, I've got a solid plan with our attorney and feel pretty confident that he'll negotiate seven years. I shift my shoulder, feeling the residual sting from my new tattoo. Like the other men in the family, I placed it over my right shoulder and down the bicep giving me a half sleeve. *BM* is written in ancient script lettering, but I placed it within an intricate Tribal design. Shane is a seriously talented artist—I'll give him that. He also added Eve's name within the lines of the bands. It's unnoticeable to anyone other than me, but I wanted to feel her on my skin.

Eve's hair. Eve's lips. Eve's body. Eve's smile.

I lift my head up, praying for the strength I'll need to pull this off.

CHAPTER 24

EVE

Vincent is going to prison. My heart thumps.

There has to be another option.

Even if I move to California, there's still no way I would move on from him. How could I? I've given him everything of me—my entire being. There is no Eve without Vincent.

I stare down at my bruised body, hoping that whatever it was he needed from me, he got. Deep down, I know he wanted to scare me. He wanted me to see him as a hardened criminal. He wanted me to run away from him. Did he think he would scare me off with his strength, size, and aggression? Too bad.

I take my time to wash up and get dressed, gently soaping my sore body. I let myself cry for twenty more minutes before I force myself to toughen up. Vincent doesn't want me to be weak. He wants me to be strong. If he goes to prison, I want him to know that I can be a support for him. The first thing I need do is head over to the law library and make some sense of his predicament. Right now, I refuse to dwell. I'm going to invest all of my energy on the present moment, which is gathering knowledge about Vincent's situation. The more I know, the more control I'll have.

I leave the apartment, trying not to look at anything too hard as I make my way to the door. Every single square inch is full of memories; I don't want to start crying again. I stop at a corner deli and pick up a coffee and a toasted butter bagel before jumping onto the subway, heading back uptown to school. The train is full of people, but luckily, I squeeze into a spot where I can hold onto the pole. I flinch as my hand touches the cold metal, thinking about the article in *High and Low* that started everything.

Finally, I'm at my stop. I walk to campus with my head down, deep in thought. I've already missed a day of classes; one more won't kill me.

The law school library stands dauntingly at the top of a hill. I enter with soft steps, but I can still hear the echo of my shoes against the floor. Another woman may be overwhelmed by the gothic architecture and high stacks, but I'm not ordinary. If there is an answer to helping Vincent, I'm damn well going to find it.

I begin by scouring the internet for cases on the American mafia. I compile a list of keywords, including RICO. Once I've done enough of that cursory research, I find one of the librarians, explaining to her that I'm trying to get information on previous cases where the defendants were indicted under RICO. After a fifteen-minute crash course on how to search case law, I begin.

I review every court case I can find on the topic, reading and then re-reading in order to capture the details. So many of the results of these cases are simply changed based on what facts the federal government can prove. It's obvious now why Vincent is pleading to a lesser charge. If the Borignones were ever found guilty under RICO, they would be forced to forfeit everything the family has made under the assumption that all the money is somehow tainted from their illegal dealings. With just an indictment of RICO alone, the government can freeze all of their assets and property. Hours pass, and the reality only becomes clearer. Vincent has no choice but to plead guilty—to something other than racketeering. I feel sick.

Time continues to move at too fast of a pace. I'm sure I'd be better able to help Vincent if I weren't in the dark when it came to his business dealings.

Lifting up my head, I blink. I turn my gaze toward the window, surprised that it's already dark. I blink and rub my eyes that feel like sandpaper from hours of crying and reading. My phone rings—it's a number I don't recognize.

"Hello?"

"Hello, I'm looking for Eve Petrov." A professional sounding voice comes across the line, and I swallow away the rasp in my throat.

"Yes, this is she."

"Good afternoon. This is Anna from Mr. Farkas's office. I'm calling to see if you're available for an interview tomorrow morning at ten thirty. He can meet you at 347 Fifth Avenue, Suite 302, across from the Empire State Building."

"My interview?"

"Yes. Your interview with the Mr. Farkas of the admissions committee at Stanford." Her voice sounds annoyed, and my mouth runs dry. "Ms. Petrov, are you still on the line?"

"Y-yes," I stammer. "I'm here."

"I know it's last minute, but another candidate canceled while I was reviewing your file. I'm glad the timing works for you. Goodbye." She clicks off. My mind is spinning so quickly; I can barely form a coherent thought.

I inhale and exhale, attempting to get my bearings. I need to weigh the risks and benefits of staying here in New York City versus leaving. For one, if Vincent's enemies do find out about me, my life could be in jeopardy. On the other hand, I don't want us to break up. I can write letters from California—wherever. The thought of losing him—no! I can't even think of it. I breathe deeply. I need to go see Vincent and tell him about my interview and everything I've learned based on previous case law. Maybe once he knows I've agreed to leave the city, he won't force me away from him. Maybe I can help him to win this case. Or, appeal.

I shut the books in front of me and take care in putting them back where they belong. I pull my purse off the wooden desk and it hits the floor with a clang.

I get down to SoHo and square my shoulders, stepping off the subway. It's a cool night, but my excitement is keeping me warm. For a moment, I pause, wishing I had a better plan of what to say. Maybe I should stop by the corner deli, grab a coffee and a cookie, and plan my words. I'm debating my next move when a group of girls enter the building. They strut into the lobby, and for reasons I don't completely understand, I follow straight behind them.

They're in skirts so short, I can see the bottom of their asses. They're wearing sky-high heels and chunky rhinestone jewelry; add in fake tits and red lips, it's clear they're walking sex.

My heart pounds.

We enter the elevator together and I listen to them talk about a girl named Alessandra, and whether or not she brought the party favors. It doesn't take much to guess what they're referring to. I've never seen girls like this in this building; it's strange.

The elevator stops at the fifth floor, and we step out together. One of them flips her bleached blonde hair to the side and reaches into her bra to push her boobs up, instantly giving her the look of larger cleavage. I'm standing there, feeling like a ghost. They don't notice me, and I'm completely silent.

They strut to apartment 5B and I ask myself if I'm dreaming. I stare at the apartment number on the outside of the door. This is it. This is our home. I finally gain the courage to step inside.

The apartment is filled with smoke and loud music. Bodies are everywhere. Half-clad girls dance throughout the space, some dancing on top of our coffee table. Where is Vincent?

I see a man with a buzzed head. I move forward through the crowd quickly and touch his shoulder, my heart skittering in my chest. When he turns around, I suck in a hard breath. It's a complete stranger. The man looks big, dirty, and tough. Biting a cigar and staring me up and down, he chuckles. "Hey, baby."

I turn and walk forward, entering the kitchen that is now littered with bottles and cigarette butts. It looks like people are blowing lines near the stove—each taking turns bending down, holding one nostril as they inhale hard.

"Eve?" A hand grabs my elbow and I spin around. It's Tom. "What the fuck are you doing here?" His voice has no inflection, but I can see the anger pulsing at his neck. His bloodshot eyes tell me he's halfway to gone.

"W-where's Vincent?"

He laughs sardonically, his hand still wrapped around my wrist like a vise. "You shouldn't be here."

"Please, Tom. I know he's leaving. I just need to speak to him. For just a minute." I'm talking too fast, the desperation in my voice obvious. At this point, I'd beg on my hands and knees if I had to.

"Do you have any idea how much you have fucked up our lives?" His voice rises in volume. "I warned you months ago, and now because of you, not only is my best friend going to jail, but I have to accompany him there. You couldn't just keep your legs shut, huh? You had to tempt him with your 'I'm so innocent' act. Well, fuck you! You deserve whatever happens next. Do me a favor and don't transfer. Stay right the fuck here where the wolves will chew you up." He drops his head, spitting at the ground in front of me.

What have I done?

He lets me go and I make my way into the corridor, my pulse rapidly beating. There's a couple by our bedroom door, practically fucking against the wall. Who are these people? Is this Vincent's other life? It feels like I'm walking through a nightmare.

I push open the bedroom door.

My eyes immediately lock with Vincent's.

He's sitting on our bed with his pants unbuttoned. Without a shirt, his tan wide chest is on display; from his right shoulder down to his bicep, I see an intricate tattoo. One hand is on a bottle of vodka, and the other makes its way up the shoulder of a blonde. He pushes her down to her knees. I hear her exclaim, "Finally!"

I stumble backward, the wall catching my fall.

Vincent chuckles. "Well, well. What do we have here? You came to say goodbye? See me off?" He looks down at the girl. "Did I say you can stop?" He grabs the back of her hair as she eagerly pulls his pants down to his ankles, leaving him in nothing other than his black briefs.

"Vincent?" My voice cracks along with my heart. "This c-c-can't be. No." I shake my head from side to side.

"Didn't I tell you we were finished? Get out of my apartment."

I feel bile rise up my throat. I must be losing my mind, because the next thing I know, I'm trembling and nodding at the same time. The room feels smaller as my breathing accelerates. "V-Vincent? P-please…" Tears blur my vision as I sink to the wooden floor. This can't be real. I hear laughter. This isn't him. This isn't me. Who am I? The girl turns to me, licking her lips. Her hands spread on his thighs.

I move my gaze, noticing that his eyes look dead. If I didn't know any better, I'd think it was Antonio Borignone sitting on the bed before me. I stand up, tearing his cross off my neck and pulling his keys out of my bag, throwing them across the room. For a moment, I notice the stricken look in his eyes, but I'm too distraught myself to care. I run through his apartment, and out the door.

I find a cab to take me back to campus. I'm hysterically crying, and it's ugly. Tears blur my vision. I throw some cash to the driver as I exit the car. I vaguely realize that people are stopping to stare at me, but I couldn't care less. Somehow, I take out my phone to call Janelle. I can do nothing but cry into the phone.

I get to my dorm room and immediately collapse to the floor; I can't make it the few feet to my bed.

Janelle shows up. I must not have locked it, because she walks right inside the door. Dropping down to her haunches, she immediately hands me two pills. I swallow them down without any water. Minutes pass, and I feel like I'm floating above myself. We move to my bed, where I tell her everything. She shushes me, combing back my hair with her hands.

"And tomorrow is my interview with Stanford. I was supposed to be there while Vincent was in Nevada. To be closer to him."

"Don't worry, Eve." Her voice is soothing and understanding. "It's for the best. You need to leave here. Vincent is right. It's not safe for you."

"I'm dying, Janelle."

"No, sweetie. You aren't dying. Your heart's just broken."

CHAPTER 25

VINCENT

The moment Eve stumbles out of my apartment, I stand up and button my pants, throwing the girl off me. There's no fucking way I'd touch her. The last woman I'm going to feel is Eve. Only Eve. I stalk out of the bedroom door, shirtless, and pound on the wall. "Everyone, get the fuck out!" I yell. People scatter like rodents.

I get back into my bedroom and take out a small envelope from my desk drawer. Picking up my necklace off the floor, I kiss the cross and drop it inside. I'll give it to Angelo for safekeeping while I'm away. This necklace doesn't belong to me anymore.

JESSICA RUBEN

CHAPTER 26

EVE

I wake up to people loudly whispering in my room. I see Janelle in a pair of my pajamas—and Angelo. His dark hair is slicked back. He's pacing my room.

They turn together when they see I'm no longer sleeping, and Angelo steps to me. "Oh, Eve. Oh, God." Tears fill his eyes. "I never shoulda let you come here. I didn't think he'd see you. I didn't know. I shoulda told ya that Vincent was here. Oh, Eve." He drops next to me, the tightening in my chest excruciating. "After all your hard work! We can't let you lose it. Come on. Let's get you washed up, and then we're leaving."

"L-leaving?" My voice croaks.

"Yes. Your interview with Stanford is in two hours. If everything goes well, and they accept you, you'll go out there."

"But, Vincent..." I say his name and the tears begin again. I know in my heart he was only trying to push me away. He just has to hear me out that I'll leave to the West Coast. I can forgive him for last night, right?

"Eve." Angelo clears his throat. "There's something you need to know. Now, you know I'd never lie to you, right?"

I nod my head and see Janelle staring at me. Her eyes are wide and sad.

"Eve, Vincent has been with tons of women this year. Your sister filled me in on what happened between you guys." He takes a deep breath. "He was lying to you, doll."

"No. That was all just for show. He only pretended to be with Daniela." I move my eyes to my sister, who stares at me with absolute pity on her face.

Angelo touches me compassionately with a warm hand on my shoulder. "No, doll. Not for show. Three weeks ago, he was at one of the clubs getting a blow job from one of the waitresses in the bathroom. Take a look at Daniela's social media accounts. He has been with her, too, quite a lot. They were never exclusive, but I know for a fact he's been with her. And recently, they've been together more than ever."

"That's impossible!" I say vehemently. "No. He just shows up to take pictures when she needs them. He just—"

"No, sweetheart." His face turns ashen. "I'm telling you the truth." I look down at Angelo's trembling hand. "You trust me, don't you? Open your social media accounts. See for yourself. None of what you see are lies, doll."

I finally open up my social media, the same ones I've been avoiding for months. Typing in DANIELA COSTA into the search box—what comes up is enough to make me sick. It's all here, in color.

Vincent is a liar.

CHAPTER 27

EVE

Surprisingly, the interview with Stanford goes amazingly well. Janelle gave me a Xanax while we headed over to Mr. Farkas's office; that shit works wonders. By the end of the interview, he actually shook my hand and with a wink, told me he's looking forward to seeing me in the fall, as a full-scholarship student.

The only thing left to do is finish off my semester as quietly as possible and find a way to reorganize my grants. Ms. Levine forwarded me an e-mail with all of the grant information on it. I should be able to contact everyone and let them know about the move.

Angelo brings me back to my dorm where he hands me off to Janelle. I hug him goodbye and then step into her arms, immediately crying again. We binge watch *Sex and the City* and fall asleep to Carrie screaming at Big to stop fucking up her life.

I wake up alone. Janelle must have left to work. For a moment, before my mind fully wakes, I breathe easily. But then, I take the phone off my side table, scrolling through today's headlines:

Mafia Boss, Intellectual scholar, and Scheming Mastermind Vincent Borignone Pleads Guilty.

Vincent is going to prison. Seven to ten years.

CHAPTER 28

EVE

I move my brain onto automatic. I have eight more weeks of school until finals, and then I'll head out to California. I put on a pair of comfortable sweats and grab my backpack. The second I enter the dining hall to get myself some coffee and a bagel, the entire room gets quiet. I glance around, knowing something is coming. Luckily, for me, I'm in too much emotional pain to even care. All I can think about is getting out of this city.

Daniela steps up to me, all long legs, skinny jeans, and loose sweater. She takes the coffee out of my hand and spills the hot liquid over my head. I gasp as the scalding wetness seeps straight through my hair, down to my clothes, and onto my pants.

"Oops," she enunciates every letter. The dining hall is so quiet, I can hear someone in the back clearing their throat.

"Does everyone see this girl?" she yells and every single person turns their head; it's a collective gaze. "This girl fucked Vincent behind my back. Ruined his life. Told the Feds lies to get him in jail, because he wouldn't be with her. Let's all make sure to give Eve Petrov a little extra attention, huh?"

I hear gasps.
My life is falling apart.

CHAPTER 29

EVE

One month later

My last final came and went yesterday. I'm shocked to have completed my first full year of college. Angelo is on his way to take me to the airport, and I still have a few odds and ends to pack. Although I insisted I could get to California on my own, he surprised me with two tickets to San Francisco International Airport. From there, we'll rent a car and drive the thirty minutes to Stanford. He said he needed a vacation anyway, but I know that he just wants to make sure I'm settled and comfortable. Luckily, Stanford is allowing me to begin over the summer, which is quite a relief. At the rate I'm going, I'll be able to graduate from college in only two more years.

Saying goodbye to Janelle and Claire was difficult, but necessary. The past two months have been excruciating. Janelle has tried to come over as often as she can, but it's difficult with her schedule. Claire and I still chat, but it isn't easy for her when I've become the most hated girl on campus.

Daniela managed to spread every vile rumor possible about me. Not only am I called a whore to my face, but people are actually saying that I fuck guys for tuition. People seemed to think it was funny to *accidentally* spill food or drinks all over my clothes or head. It didn't take long for me to realize that while I was no longer in the middle of the ghetto afraid for my life, the people here can be just as terrifying. The entire school now sees me as a slut. I'm the girl who put Vincent Borignone behind bars.

Vincent's warnings about his rivals finding out about me still knock around in my head. But I guess Daniela was good for something; the rumors she spread make it pretty clear that I'm not his ex-lover, but a bona fide enemy. I wouldn't be surprised if the Cartel sends me a goddamn fruit basket at this point.

I pull my stringy hair back with a tie, unconcerned with the fact that I haven't worn makeup in months and I haven't washed my hair since last Saturday. The only thing I care about now are grades and moving on with my life.

One thing is for sure: the world doesn't owe me shit. But, I'm prepared to work hard and succeed at my goals. I still intend on going to law school after I finish my undergraduate degree. None of my plans have to change.

I'm still working through the fact that Vincent and I are totally done. While I do think we had love, he always made it clear that there was another side to him. I guess I was too dumb and blind to notice. I wish I had someone to really talk to about it all. But the truth is, no one can relate to what happened to me. Talking about it is nothing but futile. I just want to bury my feelings, along with the memory of him. It's too painful to deal with.

That's not to say I haven't had compulsive conversations with him in my head. They go something like this:

"Vincent! Why? How could you do that to me?"

"I just wanted to know what it felt like to have someone at home."

Or, other times, he'd say:

"I just couldn't control my urges; I'm a sexual man, and I was never willing to say no to a woman."

And every so often, he'd say:

"No baby. I made Angelo lie. I had to save you from my enemies. I had to make sure you had no hope left so that everyone knew we were over."

Somehow, I vaguely remember him whispering something about art the night he came home before he broke things off. But for the life of me, I can't remember what he was talking about. But what good would it do, anyway? He wanted me gone, and he got his wish.

I look around my now-empty dorm room. I can't believe that only a few hours ago, this space was filled with books and clothes, and now, it's completely abandoned and empty. It's oddly wistful.

I can smell Angelo coming down the hall and let out a quiet laugh. Finally, he steps inside, placing a warm hand on my back. "Ready, sweetheart?"

Somehow, his scent makes me feel secure. I take a deep breath before handing him two pieces of luggage to bring down to the car.

***

LaGuardia Airport is mayhem, but Angelo and I make it to the gate with a few minutes before boarding. Before we get onto the plane, I stuff my hand in the small zipper pocket inside my purse, trying to find a piece of gum. I feel something hard. I pull it out and lift it closer to my face to inspect it. It's a silver boot charm.

"What is this?"

I hand it to Angelo, and he looks at it. "It looks like a boot."

"No shit," I laugh. "But why is this here?"

He chuckles. "How the hell am I supposed to know? You girls have tons of random junk in your bags." For a moment, I remember Claire's gigantic bag, and I smile.

But of course, my mind starts racing. The only charms I've ever had were from the keychain Vincent gave me. But, why is it here? Could it have fallen off the chain? Maybe Vincent had something to do with this—did he remove it off the keychain? Was he trying to tell me something? I swallow back tears as I get on the plane. My mind is probably playing tricks on me, looking for anything as a sign of hope.

I walk onto the flight, handing my ticket to the stewardess. She smiles kindly, gesturing to my seat.

I pause, turning around to Angelo behind me. "You didn't have to get us first class."

"Of course, I did. Your first time flying, gotta be the best." He winks at me, but I can see the sadness behind the smile. Even though I love him, I feel this inexplicable urge to push him away. Maybe leaving really was the right move. I need to start over. I can't face my past anymore.

California, here I come.

ACKNOWLEDGEMENTS

I am indebted to the following people for their help and support:

To Jon, you're the one I live for.

To my beautiful children, who give my life meaning.

To Billi Joy Carson at Editing Addict.

To Ellie at Love n' Books.

To Autumn at Wordsmith Publicity, who put my name on the map.

To Sarah at Okay Creations for the gorgeous cover.

To Leigh Ford, my Master Beta Reader.

To Andrea at Hot Tree Editing.

To Candice, Jana, Jayme, Amee and Roxy, for your amazing feedback.

ENJOYED WHAT YOU JUST READ?
YOU CAN CHECK OUT ALL OF MY BOOKS HERE!

www.amazon.com/JESSICA-RUBEN/e/B07CNNNCC1/ref=ntt_dp_epwbk_0
P.S.- They're all FREE with Kindle Unlimited!

Books in the Vincent and Eve series:
Rising (Vincent and Eve Book 1)
Reckoning (Vincent and Eve Book 2)
Redemption (Vincent and Eve Book 3)

Want to know about all the sales, updates, or news I have? Sign up for my newsletter
www.jessicarubenauthor.com/newsletter/

Interested in hanging out with me and chatting all things books? Join my Facebook group, Jessica's Jet Setters
www.facebook.com/groups/611871522504882/?ref=br_rs

Printed in Great Britain
by Amazon